A
Harlequin
Romance

Peggy Clark

HEAVEN IS HIGH

by

ANNE HAMPSON

HARLEQUIN BOOKS   TORONTO
WINNIPEG

Original hard cover edition published in 1970
by Mills & Boon Limited, 17-19 Foley Street,
London   W1A 1DR, England

© Anne Hampson 1970

Harlequin edition published March, 1972

SBN 373-01570-4

Reprinted August, 1972

Printed in Canada

CHAPTER I

The lovely black and white mansion stood on a rise over-looking a lake and the ancient village church. It was the capital house of the Manor of Marbeck in Cheshire, and had been occupied by only five families since the days of the Normans.

Its history was being recited to a group of interested visitors by Kathryn Ramsey who, when she had finished, smiled and inquired if anyone had any questions to ask.

'I have.' A tall, grey-haired man came forward out of the crowd, followed by his wife. 'It doesn't concern anything you've been telling us, Miss Ramsey, but as you know, my wife and I come often to the Hall—it's just a nice afternoon's run for us—and we're naturally anxious to know whether we'll still be able to come when the new owner takes over.' He glanced around. 'I expect there are others who come here regularly and would like to know whether the house is still going to be open to the public.'

Kathryn was shaking her head. She explained that she knew no more than they. All she did know was that an heir had been found, an American who might like to live here but, on the other hand, he might prefer to sell the property and return to his home in the United States.

'If he does decide to stay there's no certainty that he'll keep it open, is there? He might want to keep it private.'

'Can't afford to these days,' someone called out from the back. 'Poor as can be, these gentry; taxed so as they can't scarcely live. All stately homes are open to the public, and I think whoever comes here will carry on just as usual.'

'I hope so,' another voice said, and several others echoed the same wish.

' I've been coming ever since it opened, six years ago.'

And she had been here that long, Kathryn mused a few minutes later when the visitors had drifted out to wander over the lovely grounds. She was seventeen when, on answering the advertisement, she had been interviewed by the rather ferocious-looking lord of the manor. Mr Southon was considering opening Marbeck Hall to the public, and Kathryn had known instantly that though the money might be an inducement, Mr Southon's chief desire was for this ancient and historical house to be open to all who cared to come and enjoy its beauty. He had asked Kathryn numerous questions, and so great was her knowledge of the history of Cheshire that he had declared that she knew more about his house than he! Promptly he had engaged her as guide, but almost from the first she had been given the duties of secretary to Mr Southon. Then more and more responsibility had been placed upon her as her employer's health began to fail until, in the end, she was practically running the place for him. Six months ago he had died and Kathryn was still waiting to see how this would affect her own position.

At first it was thought that no heir existed, but a thorough examination of some ancient papers had brought to light the fact that one of Mr Southon's ancestors had emigrated to America and now an heir had been traced.

Many were the times Kathryn had speculated on this man's character and appearance. The newspapers had given a graphic picture of a weather-beaten uncouth cowhand who would be so like a fish out of water in the lovely manor house that he would immediately sell out and return to his own country.

Well, thought Kathryn, she wouldn't have long to wait now, for she had heard from the solicitor that Mr John Hyland would be arriving in England in just over three weeks' time.

When at last the visitors had gone Kathryn went round closing all the windows in that part of the house which was on view to the public. A young student, one of a group who came at the week-ends to help, entered the Green Room and began to assist her.

'Have the others gone?' she asked in surprise. 'I haven't paid them.'

'They were in a hurry—going to a party, and said they'd get their money tomorrow.'

'Brian doesn't come on Sundays—but I expect one of the others will take it for him.'

'I think it's all safe now, Miss Ramsey,' he said ten minutes later. 'I've been upstairs.'

'Thank you, Paul. Oh, I've an idea there's one open in the Chapel; I'll go and see to it.'

'I've done that,' he smiled, moving to the door. 'Goodbye, Miss Ramsey, I'll see you tomorrow.'

Despite the young man's assurance Kathryn went upstairs and examined all the windows. Then, satisfied, she went through the Gallery leading to the private part of the house and into the large but cosily-furnished sitting-room. Her two sisters were there, with several of their young friends. Dawn was sprawled out on the rug in front of the empty fireplace; Rita was on the couch with her boy-friend, and Phil, one of Dawn's boy-friends, was over in the corner by the record player.

'What shall we have now?' he was saying, a record in his hand.

'Nothing, please, Phil,' Kathryn put in. 'I want a little peace.' She came into the room, closed the door behind her and added, 'By the way, don't have it so loud in future. It can be heard in the Library.'

'So what?' Rita said pertly. 'It's nice music.'

'That's a matter of opinion,' Kathryn returned smoothly, and then, 'I could do with a cup of tea. Is anybody making one?'

'I will,' Dawn offered, jumping up. 'Phil, come

and help me, there's a pet.'

A moment later Kathryn followed her sister into the kitchen.

'Will you leave us, Phil? I have something to say to Dawn.'

'Of course.'

Kathryn waited until the door closed after him, then she turned to regard Dawn severely, her grey eyes kindling with suppressed anger.

'This can't go on, Dawn. I allowed you and Rita to come here, but I'm not having these crowds in every evening and week-end. You seem to forget this is not my house. Have you thought what would happen were the new owner to come here now?'

'Well, he won't come here now. You've had definite word from the lawyers that he's coming at the end of the month, so why the fuss? In any case, from what he seems to be like he'll not have the courage to object.'

Dawn was right there, Kathryn had to admit. If the papers' description of him were correct he'd be too over-awed to say much at all.

'It must stop, nevertheless,' Kathryn insisted firmly. 'Don't bring them here again.'

A pout came to Dawn's pretty lips and she glanced reproachfully at her sister.

'But, Kate, it's our home and we've got to have our friends. We go to theirs—'

'It's not your home,' Kathryn flashed angrily. 'How can you talk such nonsense?'

'Well, you said we could stay here.'

'Not indefinitely; only until you found another flat. But you're not looking.' She almost reminded her that she and Rita wouldn't have been turned out of the flat they had if the rent had been paid regularly, but she refrained. 'You'll have to find somewhere, quickly. And when you do,' she added warningly, 'see that you pay your rent before you begin spending on clothes and all the other things you don't need.'

'Oh, Kate, stop preaching!' Dawn snatched the tea caddy from the shelf and took off the lid. 'You're always at us. I suppose it's because you're so old.'

This brought a faint smile to Kathryn's lips. She had certainly felt old since that day when, rashly, she had consented to having her two young sisters staying at the Hall. Not only were they living rent free, but neither had yet offered anything towards her board, and they had been here for almost four months.

'I'll tell you frankly, Dawn, I regret having allowed you to come in the first place. I certainly wouldn't have done so had I known you'd stay as long as this.'

'Don't worry. If we don't get somewhere before he comes we can always go back home.'

'You're optimistic,' retorted Kathryn with a lift of her brows. 'Why do you think Mum and Dad told you to be off in the first place? Because you were a nuisance, with all your rowdy friends—to say nothing of the way you were both forever borrowing from them.' She shook her head. 'No, they won't have you, so you'd better begin looking at once.'

'Oh, very well! But don't keep on so. We'll find somewhere.'

'And in the meantime keep that crowd away.'

Dawn's eyes widened in dismay.

'Rita's party—her birthday; you can't expect her to give everyone back word. Please, Kate, just this once?'

'Very well, just this once.' Kathryn gave a resigned little sigh and went back to the sitting-room.

When she had finished her tea she went out, over to the clearing by one of the five lakes that were included in the beautiful grounds of the Hall. The grass was soft and springy beneath her feet and the evening sun was warm on her arms and legs. How she loved this place! A little pang of uncertainty took the pleasure out of her walk, for she was so afraid that the new owner would

9

sell out and that someone would come who wouldn't require her services. Or, should the new owner decide to stay, he might not want to open the house to the public; there was no real necessity for doing so, for not only was the estate prosperous, but Mr Southon had left a considerable fortune.

Seven caravans were spaced neatly along one side of the lake and as she reached the first one Kathryn smiled and stopped for a moment, chatting to the old couple sitting in their deck chairs on the grass.

' How are you both? Everything all right?'

' Fine, Miss Ramsey.' The old woman returned her smile, but when she again spoke there was a hint of regret in her voice. ' We shan't want to be moving, dearie. It's so lovely here.'

' You'll have to, though,' Kathryn warned. ' I believe the site will be ready for you in about a fortnight's time.'

' It won't be as nice as this—'

' Now, Mother, don't you be ungrateful,' her husband interposed severely. ' Miss Ramsey's been very good to let us all come. If she hadn't, I don't know where we'd have been when the site closed down so unexpectedly. We knew it was only until the new site is ready,' he went on, wagging a finger at his wife. ' We don't want to be here when the new owner arrives—and get Miss Ramsey into trouble, now do we?'

' Of course not, Will.'

Kathryn moved on to the end caravan. Mrs Percival was eighty-two and all alone in the world. She had three major ailments including a very weak heart. Yet she had the spirit of an eighteen-year-old and would, she declared, never enter either a hospital or a home.

' I want to be found here, in my van,' she had told Kathryn on several occasions. ' I'll do for myself till the end. It's hell getting up in the morning, with this arthritis, and having to rest now and then because of the old heart, but I say, " Come on, Liz, up Guards an' at 'em!" and there you are, I'm on my feet.'

She was sitting on the settee, watching the wrestling, and for a few moments Kathryn dared not speak.

' Look—whoosh! That's him finished. Down he goes —out!' Mrs Percival glanced quickly at Kathryn, smiled, then turned her attention to the television again. ' It was so good of you to have electricity connected up for us,' she said absently. ' It's the wrestling, I can't do without—oh, look! That's a very technical hold, you know— Come on—oh, that woman in the front row hit him with her bag! I'm glad, I don't like this one!'

Kathryn was rocking with laughter and at last Mrs Percival dragged her gaze away from her set and joined in, her blue eyes twinkling with merriment.

' There's no technique about it at all,' Kathryn said. ' It's all for show. One man just stands there and the other picks him up and throws him on the floor. Why doesn't he get out of the way?'

' You don't understand it, dear,' the old lady returned. ' It's very technical when you get to know all the holds and things.'

' You're a tonic,' declared Kathryn. ' I'm going to miss you.' A frown crossed her brow as she watched the old lady's chest. She could actually see the violent throbbing of her heart. What courage to live with such pain! She fought to live—yet was not in the least afraid to die. ' How have you been today? The pain . . .?'

' One of my good days, in fact. One of those days when I look out at the trees and the birds and the lovely blue sky and think I'm lucky to be alive and enjoying all these things.' She smiled and told Kathryn to turn the television off. ' Never mind me; how are you? You look tired.'

' I'm not really.'

' But worried? You mustn't be. You'll know soon now how you stand. It must be causing you anxiety, not knowing what he'll be like, and whether he'll want to keep you on. It said in my paper the other day that he's a cowboy; lived in a hut all his life— Probably never washes! Just imagine, he'll not know how to go on in a place like this. A cowboy as lord of the manor —it's a wonder those Fittons don't turn in their graves!'

'He'll sell out, most likely.' Kathryn gave an unhappy little sigh. Her love for the Hall couldn't have been more intense had it been her own ancestors who had occupied it for hundreds of years. 'If he does sell I expect I shall have to leave.'

'But you can stay for a while? It's in the will—so I've heard?'

'Mr Southon provided for me to remain here for twelve months after his death. Six months have gone already. And if the new owner sells out I can't stay then, of course.'

'You're allowed to stay only if this cowboy fellow keeps the place on?'

'Yes; and then only for six months—unless he wants me to remain indefinitely, that is.'

'Such a pity it's an American. Can't have any feeling for the place—and a cowboy; I can't get over that, Miss Ramsey. He won't be educated—not living wild in those Rocky Mountains. I've been there, you know.'

'There aren't many places you haven't been to, Mrs Percival. I quite envy you.'

'Well, it was an achievement in my day, because girls didn't travel. They just got married and had babies. I didn't like that idea, so off I went, signed on a ship as a nurse—' She broke off, laughing. 'Didn't know the first thing about nursing, but I wanted to get to Africa. Luckily for me no one was ill on the voyage.'

Kathryn glanced at her watch.

'I must go.' Reluctantly she rose to her feet. 'I've the accounts to do from Sunday. We've had over sixty thousand visitors this summer up till now.'

'That's good. Must have made a lot of money.'

'Not bad at all.' Kathryn stood looking down at the electric fire for a moment and then, 'About the removal of your van, Mrs Percival, you mustn't worry—'

'Well, I was worrying, dear, because it's such an up-heaval—my old heart, you know. It does play me up if I get even the least bit excited.'

'That's what I mean; you're not to worry about a thing. I shall come and pack everything, and I'll take you to the new site in the car. You're not going to have any worry at all over it, right?'

'Right. You're nice, Miss Ramsey. And I was going to ask you what you'd done to your hair. You haven't been ruining it with that bleach, I hope?'

'It's the sun,' Kathryn laughed. 'It always bleaches it at the front.'

'It's very pretty—more silver than gold. And you have a lovely skin, dear—pale honey, is it?' She grinned. 'Always did get my adjectives wrong. My Billy—' She glanced at the photograph on the wall. 'My Billy used to say "What kind of a word is that?" But I say it doesn't matter so long as it gives you an idea. Yes, pale honey—must be that you're tanned with the sun—Now stop laughing—and looking at me with those great eyes.' Kathryn was still laughing and the old lady raised one thin white hand in mock impatience. 'Be off with you, I want to watch my wrestling. Put it on again for me.'

Only another week, thought Kathryn, and the house would be back to normal. An involuntary little grimace appeared on her face as she thought of the way she had allowed her sisters to move in, and then, on hearing of the plight of the old folks she had, quite spontaneously, offered them accommodation in the grounds of the Hall. Her mother as usual had accused her of being too soft, but Kathryn was made that way. She was also impul-

13

sive, which didn't help, for whenever she decided to do something she never stopped to think of the probable consequences of her action. Well, that was how she was made, and she had long since become resigned to her own impetuosity. Nevertheless, she breathed an inward sigh of relief at the knowledge that her sisters, and the caravans, would be gone by this time next week.

She was sitting in her bedroom, at the little desk, trying to write a letter, but she couldn't concentrate for the noise going on directly beneath her. Rita's birthday party. . . . Why did they have to indulge in such rowdyism? The noise down there must be deafening for it to penetrate the thick, oak-beamed ceiling of the sitting-room. After another unsuccessful attempt to continue with her writing Kathryn went downstairs, intending to request a little less noise. But when she opened the door and entered the room she couldn't help smiling as she stood there, watching what was going on.

Phil, complete with string tie, high boots and a Stetson hat, was prancing about in the centre of the room singing—or wailing seemed to be a better description—' I'm an old cowhand. . . .' Occasionally he would use an imaginary whip or lasso, and shout ' Giddy up, there, you ole mare, giddy up!' and now and then his antics brought forth even louder and more raucous peals of laughter from the two dozen or so girls and youths who were standing in a circle around him. The laughter became so infectious that Kathryn couldn't contain herself and she was forced to join in.

' Oh, Kate,' Dawn gasped, ' isn't he just too funny?'

Phil was now standing straight, waving his great hat in the air and shouting,

' Behold, your new lord of the manor! Here I am, straight from those jolly ole Rockies. . . .' His mouth suddenly gaped; the great hat shook like a leaf being blown in the wind, then fluttered down as Phil's hand dropped to his side.

14

Silence descended on the company and all eyes were fixed, staringly, on the man in the doorway. Kathryn turned, gasped, then lifted a trembling hand to her mouth.

In the few seconds before she spoke there became impressed on her mind the vision of a man immaculately dressed, a blue-eyed giant, brown-haired, with a face lean and bronzed, a mouth thin and tight with anger and a brow darkened with the same emotion.

'Who—who—h-how did you g-get in? I mean, are y-you—?' Lord, it couldn't be! But why then this expression of fury? She swallowed hard and tried again. 'You're not Mr—?' Points of blue ice froze her to instant silence as, after a slow contemptuous examination of the squirming company, his eyes came to rest on Kathryn's burning countenance.

'My name's Hyland—John Hyland. I'm looking for a Miss Ramsey.' Cold fury could be sensed beneath the deep and apparently lazy drawl. 'Take me to her, if you please.' He addressed himself to Kathryn, and if her knees were weak before they felt like jelly now.

'I'm—I'm Miss Ramsey,' she admitted, and for a moment he appeared to be bereft of speech. Then he shook his head in a gesture of bewilderment.

'There must be some mistake. I want Miss Kathryn Ramsey.'

'I'm Kathryn Ramsey.' She looked up at him unhappily, the only picture in her mind now being that of Phil's antics, the noisy amusement of the onlookers, and her own apparent enjoyment of the skit on the new owner of the Hall. Never, she realized, could she live that down. He still seemed sure there was some mistake, and with ever-increasing dismay Kathryn recalled Mr Lowry's high opinion of her. And the solicitor had said he had written to Mr Hyland telling him all about her. . . . No wonder he still doubted the evidence of his own ears.

'Perhaps you'll show me a room,' he requested at last, in a very soft voice. 'Is there someone who'll fetch my things from the car?' He possessed all the assurance of a man used to receiving attention, and Kathryn wondered where the newspapers had received their information. But Mr Lowry had said the man was from the ranching country. . . . Could it be that he *owned* ranches? He stepped back as he spoke, an indication that he wished Kathryn to precede him, which she did, thankfully closing the door behind her and breathing an almost audible sigh of relief as she did so. Surely Dawn and Rita would get rid of that crowd before Mr Hyland came down again.

'I'll get Burrows——' She broke off, a surge of anger spreading as, from behind the door, great peals of laughter rang forth. A fearful glance at her companion revealed the colour slowly rising in his face, and a little movement in his throat as if he had difficulty in controlling his wrath.

'I'm—I'm terribly sorry, Mr Hyland,' she began wretchedly. 'We weren't expecting you——'

'Obviously not.'

'Mr Lowry said you wouldn't be here till next week-end.'

His eyes, made more disconcerting by the deeper, metallic blue in their depths, flickered over her for a second before he repeated his request to be taken up to his room.

'Of course.' On reaching the entrance hall Kathryn rang the bell and within a few moments Burrows appeared. 'Mr Hyland's suitcases are in his car; will you take them up to the Hall Room?' she said, noting his sudden start of surprise at her words. A smile of welcome then came to his lips and he seemed about to speak to the new owner of the Hall. But, as if warned by Kathryn's expression not to make any comment at this time, he merely nodded and went out to the car.

'This way, Mr Hyland.' Still flustered by his untimely appearance, and crushed by his manner, Kathryn
led him through the dining-room towards the wall staircase which led to those rooms not on view to the public.
How could the mistake have occurred? she wondered,
unable to believe that Mr Lowry could have erred over
the date of John Hyland's arrival. No, he must have
changed his plans, she decided. And he obviously
hadn't informed Mr Lowry, for had the solicitor known
of his arrival in England he would have made sure
Kathryn had ample warning of when to expect him.
Also, Mr Lowry had said only last week that when the
new owner did arrive he himself would bring him to the
Hall and personally introduce them to one another. How
different that would all have been, thought Kathryn, her
footsteps flagging as she led the way upstairs.

'Mind your head,' she warned mechanically. The
beautiful cut-glass chandelier hung rather low, and John
Hyland was of much more than average height.

A narrow staircase led off from the Gallery, through
which they were now walking, and Kathryn gestured
towards it.

'There are two priest holes up there,' she murmured,
not at all with the confidence she had acquired in six
years of taking visitors over the house. 'One has a shaft
running right down to the ground floor. It's an escape
route.' He made no comment, in fact she wondered if
he had heard, for he was looking around with interest
at the paintings on the walls, at the panelling and the
massive oak beams. 'This is your room.' She opened
the door of the Hall Room and stood aside for him to
enter. He strode into the centre of the apartment and
stood looking from one window to the other. Then his
interested gaze rested on the great stone fireplace and,
watching him, Kathryn explained that it was very
ancient, dating from the end of the fifteenth century.
'There has been little change here since Sir Thomas

Fitton's day,' she went on. 'The glass and the wainscoting and the plaster work were all put in by him.' She turned as Burrows appeared carrying two large suitcases. 'Put them down there, by the cupboard.'

'Yes, Miss Ramsey. I'll go and fetch the others now.'

'Do you like the room, Mr Hyland?' she asked, and for a moment he seemed almost human as he scratched his head in indecision.

'Not particularly,' he replied at last.

'Wh-what!' She stared, bereft of further speech.

'I said, not particularly.'

'Why, it's a beautiful room, the principal bedroom. All the heads of the house used this. And many famous people in history have slept on that four-poster bed.'

'Including Queen Elizabeth,' he responded, moving over to the window.

'She didn't visit Marbeck,' Kathryn submitted, flushing at his hint of sarcasm.

'She didn't? He still scanned the view. 'My house must be unique among English stately homes.' He was looking out over the magnificent grounds to the largest of the lakes, and to the tower of the Norman church not so very far distant. 'Show me another room, please.'

'Don't you like the view?' she gasped, forgetting her recent embarrassment as she stared at his broad back in disbelief.

'The view is perfect. Another room, I said.'

Kathryn quite suddenly became hot. Drawing a deep breath, she persevered,

'This is the best bedroom in the whole house, Mr Hyland, and as I've said, it's always used by the head of the family. In the old days it was given to every distinguished visitor. The Duke of Monmouth slept here, and his father, Charles II, before him.'

Slowly he turned from the window to regard her with an icy stare that seemed to chill her very marrow.

'Miss Ramsey, I do not care if Henry VIII and all his wives slept here, I want another bedroom.'

At his insistence her throat moved visibly and she swallowed hard.

'I can't think why you don't like it—'

'I haven't said I don't like it.'

'Then why—?' She shook her head in bewilderment. 'I repeat, Mr Hyland, it's the best bedroom in—'

'Then show me the second best bedroom!' he snapped, glaring at her now from his great height.

'Yes, Mr Hyland. If—if you'll come this way.' He followed her into the Gallery again and she opened another door.

'This is the second best bedroom,' she submitted, moving to one side, allowing him to enter before her. Her nightdress case lay on the elegant and beautiful carved French bed, and her negligée was draped across the foot. On the dressing table were displayed her silver-handled brushes and comb, an elaborate ring stand in antique porcelain and several trinket boxes of ivory and mother-of-pearl. 'I can move out right away; I'll get one of the maids up here at once.'

'I suppose this is called the Blue Room—it must be.' Moving over to the dressing-table, he picked up the ring stand, examined the mark on the underneath, then returned it to its place, his glance at the same time flickering over the rest of the treasures lying there. And most odd was the expression in his eyes as they again rested on Kathryn's face.

'Yes, it is called the Blue Room,' she said. 'Does it please you, Mr Hyland?'

'Very much; but as it's occupied, you can show me another.'

Kathryn became so hot now that the colour rose and fused her cheeks.

'If this one pleases you—' she began, when he interrupted her to repeat that she could show him another, but

Kathryn ignored this, and went on, 'I'd much rather you have the Blue Room, seeing that you like it. I don't mind at all moving out.' She knew his patience had been tried, but she was totally unprepared for the fury in his deep tones as he said,

'Miss Ramsey, what is the matter with you! Show me another room, at once!'

'This is the Solar Room,' she informed him a moment later, and as it was in a state of complete chaos she had to add, though in a very small and rather frightened voice, 'One of my sisters has this room, but if you like it we can soon move her things.' Move them! It would take all night. And why, for heaven's sake, did Rita have to use the floor for her undies and her stockings? Two sweaters were flung on a chair, her dressing-gown was in a heap on the floor by the bed, and the walls— Fixed up between the beautiful fifteenth-century timbering were all Rita's pop singer heroes, and hanging from the ceiling, over a bed that looked as if it had never been made for days, hung a great hairy spider in black nylon fur.

A most awful silence followed before the new owner of Marbeck Hall said, in a dangerously quiet tone,

'Did you say *one* of your sisters?'

'Two of them are staying here. You see—' She met his wrathful, questioning gaze contritely and went on to say she had better explain.

'You better had, Miss Ramsey. I wasn't informed that my house had been taken over by a band of hooligans.'

That prevented speech for a moment; Kathryn could only stand there, miserably conscious of the scene of slovenliness and disorder and wishing fervently that she'd hardened her heart against her sisters' pleadings.

'The girls,' she began falteringly, 'they were turned out of their flat, so I said they might come here—but it was only until they found somewhere else—'

'How long have they been here?'

Kathryn bit her lip and confessed that they had been living at the Hall for the past four months.

'I didn't think they'd stay that long,' she added hastily on seeing that movement in his neck again. 'In any case, I meant to have them out by next week-end, that is, before you came.'

'You say they were turned out? Why?'

'They didn't pay their rent,' she had to admit, and kept her head averted, having no desire to witness the effect of that upon him. She at the same time recalled their conclusions—and her own—that the new master of Marbeck wouldn't have the courage to murmur a complaint even if he did arrive upon the scene before they left. How different from what they had all expected! Never for one moment had Kathryn imagined she would experience discomfiture such as this. On the contrary, she had half expected to find herself adopting a faintly condescending attitude towards the heir to the Marbeck estate. Presently she glanced up, to see a look of resignation on John Hyland's handsome face, though his eyes retained their icy gleam.

'Perhaps you'll show me a room where I can sleep, Miss Ramsey,' he said, and Kathryn began twisting her hands as she told him baldly that there wasn't one. His eyes opened very wide; he looked amazed.

'A great house like this and there's nowhere for me to sleep?'

'My other sister has the Compass Room—over here—and that completes our part. The rest is on view, and therefore can't be occupied.'

He was walking out and she followed him.

'There was a place off the Hall Room, as you called it. Wasn't that a bedroom?' He took long strides and soon he had entered the principal bedroom again. 'What's through here?'

'It was the dressing-room in the old days,' she said.

'Now it's a modern bathroom—for this room.'

'Hmm. . . .' He stood on the threshold, surveying the room. It was exquisite, in several shades of mauve, with just about everything a bathroom could have—even to a cushion on which to rest the head when lying in the bath! 'It goes with this room, you say? Yes, naturally it must.' He was eyeing the pretty jars of coloured bath salts and the sponge bag lying on the side of the bath.

'I've been using it,' she owned, lowering her head.

'I'll sleep here,' he decided, turning back into the room. 'Where's that fellow with the rest of my things—? There you are. Put that one on the bed.'

'Yes, sir.' Burrows did as he was told, then looked at his new employer. 'Welcome to your ancestral home, sir. I'm sure we all hope you'll be happy, and decide to stay with us.'

'Stay?' A faint lift of his brows. 'What makes you think I might not stay?'

A little colour came to Burrows' rugged face; he cast a quick glance at Kathryn. She felt she could have shaken him.

'I see. . . .' John Hyland glanced at Kathryn through slightly narrowed eyes. 'Yes, I do see. Er—thank you, Burrows, you may go.'

The air of him! thought Kathryn. Clearly he was used to servants and clearly he knew what sort of person they had all expected!

Those stupid antics of Phil's—and John Hyland's entrance at that particular moment. It was her own fault, though, she had to admit. Perhaps this would teach her a lesson; perhaps in future she would act less impulsively and think before taking pity on people.

John Hyland was now standing by the other window; Kathryn excused herself and went into the bathroom to collect her belongings and to put out clean towels and new tablets of soap. When she returned to the Hall Room John Hyland was scowling darkly as he turned his head.

'What the devil are those trailers doing on my land? It is my land, I take it?'

The caravans! Kathryn just stood there, looking almost stupefied. In her agitation and embarrassment she had completely forgotten about the caravans. Had anyone ever made such a disastrous start with a prospective employer? Well, whether or not he intended to carry on allowing the public access to his home he certainly wouldn't have the least desire to retain her services. And she wouldn't even insist on staying the six months, she decided, convinced as she was that her presence here could only be a source of irritation to him. Her lips quivered as she recalled how highly esteemed she was by Mr Southon. In all the six years she had worked for him nothing had gone wrong; at no time had he ever had to complain about her conduct or her loyalty. But this. . . .

'Yes, it is your land, Mr Hyland,' she began with haste as he eyed her questioningly, his scowl deepening. 'You see, they're old age pensioners, and they hadn't anywhere to go—'

'You mean Mr Southon gave them permission to come on his land?'

'No, Mr Hyland. I did. . . .'

'You did?' He it was who appeared stupefied now. 'They've come here since Mr Southon's death?' She nodded dumbly and he went on, very quietly, 'You actually took it upon yourself to sanction the siting of trailers on my land?' He still seemed incredulous—and no wonder, thought Kathryn as she began to stammer,

'They h-hadn't anywhere to go b-because their site closed down, so I—I said they could come here—just until the new site's ready. I intended having them off before you came.'

Turning his head to look over at the caravans again, he stood in wrathful silence for such a long time that Kathryn began to wonder if he had forgotten her presence. But at last he came away from the window, turning his attention to her again.

' It seems to me, Miss Ramsey, that you intended doing a good deal of clearing up, shall we say, before I came. How much have you been making from all this?'

' Nothing,' she retorted, her eyes flashing with indignation. ' I wouldn't dream of making money that way.'

' You mean to say you've taken in these boarders, and turned the place into a trailer park—all for no reward? My dear Miss Ramsey, I'm a business man, not an idiot —though you obviously expected me to be one. How much are you making on all this?' he repeated sharply.

' Nothing, truthfully,' she faltered, indignant and even angry, but at the same time admitting he had excuses in plenty for his accusations. ' I did it merely to help those old people, though I now know it was very wrong of me. As for my sisters, I knew at once that I'd made a mistake.' She looked up at him miserably, and went on to assure him that in less than a week everything would be back to normal.

' I'm not prepared to wait a week,' he snapped. ' I'll have no gypsies on my land—!'

' They're not gypsies, Mr Hyland. They're respectable old people.'

' Don't your councils find these people homes?' he wanted to know, frowning.

' They prefer caravans; they like living in a rural setting.'

' Well, they're not living in this rural setting. Get them off.'

She could only stand there, blinking at him, and he repeated the order.

' Get them off? Now?' she faltered.

' First thing in the morning.'

She put a quivering hand to her mouth, unconsciously taking a step towards him.

' There isn't anywhere for them to go.'

24

'Get in touch with the local authority.'

'Oh, I can't do that!' she exclaimed, then wished with all her heart that she hadn't.

'Why not?'

A long pause and then,

'The Council don't know they're on . . . what I mean is, it's an offence to have vans without their permission.'

'So you took the law into your own hands?'

'Had I asked permission it would have been refused, so I just let them on without asking for it.' He was plainly staggered by this admission, though he said nothing, merely waiting for some further explanation. 'I'm terribly sorry, about everything. It must seem dreadfully presumptuous of me, but at the time it worried me—their plight, I mean. You see, their old site closed down unexpectedly and they had nowhere to go. There was all this land and it didn't seem sensible to let them have that anxiety when their problem could be solved in a very simple way. It's only temporary—' He had turned away to look out again as though recalling something.

'What are those wires connected to the trailers?' he asked curiously, and Kathryn's throat went dry as she began to tell him that she had had an electricity supply taken from the summer house.

'Most of them rely on electricity for heating,' she added, in some haste, for he was facing her again and he seemed to be quite speechless by this time. But after a while he said, in that soft and dangerous tone,

'Is there anything else I should know, Miss Ramsey? If so, let me have it all, if you please.'

At first she shook her head, but then, in a voice of sudden resignation,

'Only that I've had water connected to their vans, too. You see, they're quite old—some of them, and they couldn't be expected to carry it. . . .'

CHAPTER II

Contrary to Kathryn's expectations the party was still in full swing when she came down to the sitting-room, and an angry light entered her eyes as she scanned the gathering, before going through to the kitchen where Rita and Dawn were making refreshments.

'You can leave those, and get that crowd out of here,' she said, trying to control her quivering voice. After all, it was Rita's birthday, and Kathryn didn't want to spoil it altogether.

'But, Kate—'

'Those capers of Phil's were crude, and definitely not in good taste. All that noise, and laughter, and Mr Hyland standing there; it was awful!'

'You laughed, too,' Dawn retorted. 'You know you did.' Both girls had obviously forgotten their few moments of embarrassment, for neither seemed in any way perturbed by what had happened.

'You won't be interested,' Kathryn almost snapped, 'but I'm quite sure I've lost my job!'

At that both girls stopped what they were doing and stared unbelievingly at their sister.

'Already? He hasn't wasted much time!'

Turning away impatiently, Kathryn went back to the other room and, walking over to the record player, switched it off.

'I'm sorry about this,' she said quietly, 'but you'll all have to leave. The new owner—'

'Leave, at this time? Kate, be a sport.' Phil retained the hands of the girl with whom he had been dancing. 'We haven't even got going properly yet.'

She turned on him angrily.

'Do as I say, Phil! Mr Hyland has asked me to show him over the house and he'll be down here in about half an hour. I want this room in order by then, so you can all take yourselves off, at once!' She thought vaguely that they would always consider her to be rude, but she must get them out before John Hyland put in an appearance.

Dawn and Rita came through with trays, stopping just inside the room as they saw the expressions on their friends' faces.

'What's wrong?'

'We've been told to go,' one young man informed them sullenly. 'Right in the middle of a smashing party like this. Some people do have spoil-sport relations!'

It was a good quarter of an hour before Kathryn could begin tidying up. She felt awful, despite her outward anger. After all, she had given permission for the party, and it wasn't very good manners to order the guests off the premises only an hour after it had begun. Where would they go? There was nowhere in the village, not even an inn. They would have to go into Macclesfield where most of them lived, and where Dawn and Rita had had their flat. There would be some haunt there, or some pub where they could continue the party, she told herself, trying to ease her conscience.

With the help of one of the maids, Kathryn managed to put the room into order, and she was just going to wash her face and brush her hair when John Hyland entered. A swift glance in the mirror revealed a shiny nose and hair which was awry, to say the least. Luck certainly wasn't with her today, she reflected dismally. A neat and tidy appearance would have restored at least a little of her confidence. As it was she felt he must be regarding her with some considerable disapproval. Not that it really mattered, for Kathryn was quite convinced she had lost her job. But he seemed to have forgotten some of his anger and irritation as, halting by the door for a while, he stared in surprise at the difference in the room, and in answer to his glance of inquiry she explained that the young people had gone off to continue the party in town.

'It was my sister's birthday,' she submitted, convinced he was not in the least interested, but feeling some explanation was necessary. 'They'd become rowdy, I'm afraid.'

'This, I take it, is the room which was used most by the late owner of the house?' he said, ignoring her effort to explain. He strode over to the window and looked out on to the wide and undulating lawn sweeping away from the side of the house and ending where a belt of willows fringed one of the lakes. It was a beautiful scene and, watching him, Kathryn saw his eyes flicker in admiration. Did he consider himself lucky in inheriting such a mellowed and historical house? she wondered, reflecting that at the time of the first manor house his country was not even discovered, and even when the newest part of the present Hall was being constructed America had not even begun to be colonized.

'Would you like to see over the house now?' she inquired politely as he turned back into the room again, and he nodded. 'I didn't ask if you wanted any refreshment,' she said, making no apology for the omission. He must know she had been too flustered even to think clearly. 'Perhaps you would like something now?'

'I dined on the way here, thank you,' he replied, and then, 'Is there someone who will go and do my unpacking?'

'Of course.' Another omission. She should have told him that one of the maids would do that. 'Do you wish it to be done now?'

'Please. I expect those cupboards and drawers can be used? They aren't falling apart from woodworm or anything?'

Kathryn shook her head and smiled faintly.

'They're all very ancient, but everything here is in a wonderful state of preservation. Each owner has loved this house, and all his possessions.'

'And you're wondering if I shall feel the same about it?' His brows were raised a fraction and Kathryn wondered if he was amused.

'As Burrows said, we've all hoped you would like the place and decide to stay here.' His brows went a little higher; Kathryn could almost hear him saying, 'And what difference will that make to you?'

'I most certainly intend to stay,' he assured her. 'And now, Miss Ramsey, shall we have that tour of the house which I mentioned?'

She took him into the entrance hall first, talking about the history of the house and pausing now and then to show him the weapons, some of which were very ancient, and very rare. She showed him the coat of arms of the previous owner, explaining the heraldic achievement; and was about to read out the motto in English when something made her change her mind.

'Perhaps you've read the motto,' she murmured, watching his expression.

'I have,' he returned quietly, and Kathryn gave a sigh of relief. She had felt, somehow, that he would know his Latin, but had that not been the case he would have been put in an embarrassing position—and liked her even less because of it.

'The English must have been small people,' he remarked, lightly fingering the suit of armour by the entrance door. 'Or isn't this English?'

'Yes, it's English—about 1320.'

'So old?' For the first time he seemed surprised, and, she thought, rather awed. 'Is it really as old as that?'

'It's early fourteenth century, yes. This is the resting place for a lance. See, it folds. We have a very fine tilting ground here and tournaments took place regularly—but you probably know about that?'

'I've read about it, yes.'

She then took him to the Library and he stood admir-

ing the numerous books, some very ancient and beauti-
fully bound in leather.

'The mantelpiece is Tudor—about four hundred years
old,' she said, realizing with a little shock that at the
time it was installed at the Hall there were still about
fifty years to go before those English Puritans set sail to
found the colony of Plymouth in that land of promise
across the Atlantic. 'We have proof of a Neolithic
settlement here . . . this flint axe head. It dates from
around 2000 B.C.' She went on to inform him about the
furniture and then they moved on.

'We now come to the Long Hall,' she said. 'This
table is Chippendale, from the Mayor collection, and you
will notice the pictures—these are all Morlands, and over
there—the sunset—is a Turner, and that one's a Con-
stable—' Arrested by his expression of amusement,
Kathryn stopped, flushing, and then said apologetically,
'I'm so used to explaining everything. I'll take you
round more quickly if you like?'

'Not at all,' he returned, to her surprise. 'Tell me
everything as we go along. What about these famous
Fittons?'

'Theirs was a long and splendid history,' she said,
adding that he would find it much more interesting to
read about it for himself, and confined her comments to
a brief description of some of the marvellous banquets
and jousts which had taken place when honoured guests
were in residence at the Hall.

They went into the Chapel, and the Dining-Room,
then from the Guard Room to one of the most beautiful
apartments in the whole house, the Drawing-Room.

'This was always the main living-room,' Kathryn explained as they stood by the window looking out upon
the view which, like the room itself, had remained un-
changed through four centuries of history. The massive
wall enclosing the lovely acres of parkland had been built
by Sir Edward Fitton, friend of Queen Elizabeth and of

30

whom it was said 'he has a haughty countenance and contempt of superiority'. As Kathryn related this she found herself examining John Hyland's face even more searchingly than before. He might almost have been one of those famous Fittons himself, she decided, moving away from the window.

'This fellow was the father of that Mary Fitton, the Dark Lady of Shakespeare's sonnets?' he queried, his eyes flickering with interest.

'Grandfather,' she corrected. 'Though her father was an Edward, too.'

'It isn't a certainty that she was the Dark Lady, I believe?'

'No . . . but we think it's possible. It's thought that Shakespeare stayed a while at Marbeck Hall at about that time.' She paused, waiting patiently as he went round examining the pictures with the keen and knowledgeable interest of the connoisseur.

'This—' He referred to the portrait of Anne, Lady Fitton, mother of the famous Mary and her less famous but certainly more sweet-natured sister, Anne. The children in the portrait with their mother were Mary and her brother Edward. 'The Fitton arms . . . ?' He pointed to the shield up in the corner above Mary's head.

'Sir Edward married a Holcroft—they were a very famous Cheshire family at that time—and the arms incorporate those of Holcroft.' Heavens, was he versed in heraldry, too? An amused smile came fleetingly to her lips. Those who had written so disparagingly about him were going to have very red faces before they were much older. On the way up she warned him again to mind his head. As she spoke she turned, and surprised an odd expression on his face. He was clearly convinced that her anxiety was for the priceless Waterford chandelier and not for his head!

He had seen some of the bedrooms, but Kathryn naturally did not remind him of this; instead she took

31

him to the others, answering his questions and explaining anything over which he seemed puzzled.

From the window of the Fitton bedroom—where Mary was supposed to have slept—could be seen the foothills of the Derbyshire Pennines, for the house was close to the border.

'This is the Blue Room . . . the Solar . . . the Griffin Room. . . .' And so it went on, for a long while, with John Hyland never once losing interest and Kathryn never tiring of talking about the house which she had come to love with such intensity that her heart sank at the idea of leaving it, never to return.

At last they were outside, but by now it was almost dark and after a cursory glance around the house itself John decided he had had enough. But he stood by the front door, obviously enjoying the soft June night and the scented breeze coming across from the flower-filled gardens.

'Perhaps you're now ready for a drink?' she said politely when they were back in the sitting-room. 'I don't know what you would like . . . we have a very good cellar here—' She broke off, a hint of colour rising. Why did she keep saying 'we'? It was use, she knew, but this was no time to be saying it.

'I'd like a cup of coffee,' he said, with that faint drawl which Kathryn was beginning to find attractive. 'Perhaps you'll keep me company?'

'Yes, of course.' He seated himself comfortably on the couch, his long legs stretched out in front of him, his eyes wandering around the room. He seemed either to have forgotten her presence, or was deliberately ignoring it, and Kathryn went out to prepare the coffee, which she soon brought in, along with biscuits and cakes which were attractively arranged on a silver dish.

She gave him his coffee, then sat down, on the big chair at the other end of the room. For the first time since coming here she felt awkward and unsure of herself; for the first time for years she had the feeling of not belonging, of being what she really was, a servant.

' You don't get the maids to do this?' he queried, picking up a biscuit and putting it on the plate she had given him.

' They have almost every evening free. Mr Southon insisted on that. They also have two days off each week —taking it in turns, of course, so that we always have one on duty.'

' There are only two?'

She nodded, and blinked in surprise.

' We have two daily women as well, and Burrows.' How many servants was he used to? she wondered. ' And we have—there are three gardeners.'

' What about a chauffeur? I'm informed that Mr Southon was in poor health for a long while before he died.'

' I drove him about,' she replied, and an odd light entered his eyes.

' What else did you do?'

She hesitated, wishing she could avoid an answer.

' I did all the accounts.'

' What else?'

' As you say, he wasn't in good health, so I—' She broke off, shrugging slightly. ' I did practically everything.'

' In other words,' he murmured, thoughtfully stirring his coffee, ' you made yourself almost indispensable to your employer.'

She frowned, and moved uncomfortably in her chair.

' Naturally I did all I could, but I didn't deliberately make myself indispensable to Mr Southon. His illness necessitated my taking on more and more duties as time passed. He relied on me and I helped him all I could.' Surely it must be imagination, but it did seem as if his expression were one of distrust.

' How long have you worked for Mr Southon?'

' Six years.'

'And you've lived here all that time?'

'I'd been coming two months when Mr Southon asked me to live in.' What an odd situation, she suddenly thought. Here she was, sitting with this stranger, telling him all about herself, and her work, and not knowing a thing about him. He had no wife, she knew, for Mr Lowry had told her that. But had he a family—parents and brothers and sisters? What had been his job? There were so many questions she would have liked to ask, but all she managed was an inquiry as to whether or not he intended carrying on as before and allowing the public access to his home.

'For the present, yes,' he said, picking up his cup and saucer from the little inlaid table Kathryn had placed beside him. 'You say you did all the accounts?' And, when she nodded, 'You've been keeping them then, since Mr Southon died?'

'Yes. The money has been paid into the bank, and the books go to Mr Lowry every month.'

'But expenses, and wages?—what did you do about those?'

'I stopped the money before giving it to Mr Southon.' She suddenly thought about his insinuations that she had been making money from the caravans and by having her sisters here and with a wholly involuntary gesture her chin lifted and she added, 'The books are all in order, Mr Hyland, I can assure you I'm to be trusted.'

'My good girl. . . .' He seemed quite taken aback for a space and then his brow darkened. 'I don't doubt for one moment that you're honest, Miss Ramsey.'

'I'm sorry.' No sense in worsening her position by taking offence, she chided herself. For although she felt she had lost her job, he hadn't actually said anything definite about it. And suddenly she wanted to know, one way or another, for the uncertainty had been going on for over six months. 'As you are intending to carry

34

on as usual, will you be wanting me to stay here?'

'No, Miss Ramsey. I prefer to engage my own staff.' Not a flicker of an eyelid, no sign of the hesitancy or embarrassment one would expect under such circumstances. And they had all been awaiting the appearance of a rough and ready cowhand, a rather ludicrous figure without breeding or taste who would be so out of his depth in the refinement of his new position that he would be glad to sell out as speedily as possible and return to his more comfortable environment among his own kind. Instead, here was a gentleman, cultured, confident and poised, with all the *savoir-vivre* of the aristocratic Fittons themselves.

His words, so coolly spoken, brought the colour to her cheeks. She accepted his decision—there was no alternative—but, profoundly conscious of the damaging impression he had obtained of her, she met his gaze seriously and apologized once more for the presence of the caravans, and of the girls, admitting her action in allowing them to come had been most imprudent.

'I'm glad you realize that, Miss Ramsey. It will then give you some better understanding of my decision not to retain your services. I make it a rule to keep in my employ only those people who have my interests at heart and respect my property.'

Kathryn's cheeks coloured more hotly and she lowered her head. She did not cry easily, but tears pricked the backs of her eyes now. She had grown so used to the life here, had become so steeped in the history of the Hall that she couldn't envisage herself in any other employment. She wondered if he knew of the provision made for her by Mr Southon, knew that he couldn't dismiss her for another six months. Not that it mattered, she thought, for she wouldn't dream of insisting on his strict adherence to the wishes of his predecessor. He didn't want her, and therefore she would go when he told her to. She inquired about this, in a voice that was low and clear, but certainly not very steady.

' You'll have the usual month's notice, naturally, Miss Ramsey. That can begin from the end of this week.' He paused, then changed the subject, asking when she expected her sisters to be leaving.

' They must go tomorrow,' she replied at once. ' Mother will have to take them until they find a flat.'

His blue eyes became fixed on her and for a moment she thought he intended asking for some more explicit reason as to why all this had come about, but he changed his mind and went on to inquire about the new caravan site and when it was expected to be opened.

' In about a week's time ; then they'll go immediately.' If only he had arrived when he should ! she thought again. Everything would have been orderly, giving him a far different impression. And it was reasonable to assume he would have kept her on, although he would, she felt sure, have relieved her of much of the responsibility—and the freedom of action—which she had always enjoyed with Mr Southon. ' They can stay, the old people, until next week ? ' she added, anxiously scanning his face.

' It seems they'll have to, for I now see it's impossible to get them away in the morning.' A flash of anger crossed his brow, but it was gone instantly, replaced by a look of resignation.

Silence followed and as awkwardness began to sweep over her again Kathryn asked if he wanted more coffee.

' I've had enough, thank you.'

' I'll take the tray away, then.' He watched her for a moment while she put the cups and saucers on the tray, then he said curiously,

' Didn't Mr Southon have a private sitting-room—one for his own use entirely ? '

' He spent much time in his bedroom—lying down, during the last two or three years. Until then he had this room and my room was furnished as a sort of bed-sitting-room.' She took the tray from the table and straightened up. ' If you want this room to be private I'll find another one to use.'

' It doesn't matter,' he returned shortly. ' I can arrange everything to my satisfaction as I go along.' In other words, Kathryn thought, he would tolerate her for the short time she would be here.

With the dishes washed and put away she looked in merely to say goodnight and left her new employer in sole possession of the sitting-room.

As word spread that the new owner of Marbeck Hall had taken up residence, so the number of visitors increased, for interest in the Hall and its occupants had always been great, owing mainly to its historical associations and the fact that its earliest foundations dated back to the middle of the twelfth century. In addition, it was one of the most beautiful and carefully maintained stately houses in the whole of the north of England. Adding to its interest, from the visitor's point of view, was the fact that it was lived in by the owner; for so many of these great houses were just museums, totally lacking in atmosphere and warmth. And Mr Southon had been so inordinately trusting, leaving all his treasures around, for he had a genuine love for his fellow men and wanted them to share, at least in some measure, the beautiful things which he had been fortunate enough to inherit. And now the regular visitors wanted to know what the new owner was like, and whether he would be as free and trusting as his predecessor. The difficulty in finding an heir, and the fact of his being an American, had been given much publicity. And when it was known he came from the ranching country it was rashly assumed that he worked on a ranch—that he was in fact a cowboy. How this mistake had originated no one knew, but on the appearance of the new lord of the manor it was speedily rectified. Ranching was John

Hyland's business, it was true, but it was now rumoured that he owned so much land, both in the Rockies and on the great wheat-producing central plain, that he didn't know just how much money he was worth.

To everyone's delight and satisfaction the new heir was often about during the week-ends when the Hall and gardens were thrown open to the public. He might be seen wandering in the grounds, or moving about the house, and always he would smile or nod in response to some such gesture from one of the visitors.

'This is what they like,' Kathryn had said once or twice during the first week-end. 'It brings the crowds.' Even as she spoke she wondered if he were interested in the profits from all this. He had said he was a business man, though, so she surmised that he was just as eager to make money as anyone else. As for Kathryn herself, the increased numbers meant also an increase in her own hours of work, for there was always the book-keeping to do afterwards. In addition, she spent almost every evening with her employer, answering his numerous questions, explaining how the business was run, and giving him a general idea of the workings of the estate as a whole. He meant to run it himself—as Mr Southon had done until his health began to fail—and Kathryn felt that when she had gone he would employ someone to come in at the week-ends only.

From the first his manner towards her had been cool, to say the least, and Kathryn knew he had formed the impression that Mr Southon had allowed her far more than normal privileges . . . and that she had taken advantage of them. The two girls had left the day after his arrival, and the caravans had moved off a few days later, to Kathryn's intense relief. During the week, and in the evenings, the house was now quiet, and filled with that strange atmosphere of peace that only age and mellowness can provide. John Hyland seemed to enjoy this and the only alteration he intended to make at present was the closing off completely of that part of the house in which he intended to live. As it was now, the 'Private' notices were all that kept the visitors out of his apartments.

Kathryn was leaving at the end of July and the Sunday prior to her going was expected to be extra busy, for in the early morning a heat haze hung over the Derbyshire hills, and over the lakes in the grounds of the Hall, while the pearl-like ball of the sun began to penetrate and disperse the mist, promising a perfect day.

Naturally by this time Kathryn was quite resigned to leaving, yet the prospect, ever with her, was still so dismaying that she had the greatest difficulty in maintaining the pleasant, lighthearted manner to which the regular visitors had become so used. Nevertheless, she made a heroic effort and to her relief no one seemed to notice her dejection. She had never been a guide in the sense that she took parties round the house, mechanically rattling off dates and events in the history of the Hall; she was there to comment on some picture or other beautiful object, to answer questions or direct people to any part of the Hall they particularly wanted to see. Also, she naturally kept an eye on anyone who appeared not to have the proper respect for the lovely things they were privileged to view, and also that small minority who allowed their children to run wild about the house.

She was discussing one of the paintings with Michael Robson, an antique dealer who, at only twenty-three, had already been in the business for nearly eight years. She had a great respect for his knowledge, and he for hers, and whenever he visited the Hall they would have a long and interesting discussion on the merits of one or two of the beautiful paintings displayed lavishly on every wall in the house.

John Hyland, too, was keenly interested in the paintings, and while Kathryn and Michael were talking he paused on his way through the Drawing Room to stand in the background listening to their comments. Suddenly aware of his presence, Kathryn felt a hint of colour rise, but she continued her conversation as before. When Michael discovered his presence he drew him into the conversation and in the most immodest way imaginable a wealth of knowledge poured forth from his lips. After widening in astonishment John Hyland's eyes became fixed and interested as Michael discussed the methods and technique of various painters, and when eventually he paused a look of admiration had spread across John Hyland's face. He seemed about to speak and before he did so Kathryn introduced them and then, approached by one of the students who was having difficulty in controlling some young children, she excused herself and left the two men together.

On returning about ten minutes later Kathryn found them still in conversation and was just about to join them again when she heard her name called and she turned to encounter the beaming smiles of an elderly couple, and the less cordial nod of greeting from their daughter.

' How nice to see you, Kathryn.' Mr Slade shook hands vigorously. ' We thought we'd better come along and introduce ourselves to the new owner. Is he in?'

Kathryn nodded, genuinely pleased at the appearance of the couple, but not so pleased that their daughter was with them. Mr and Mrs Slade were old friends of her late employer, and had at one time been regular visitors to the Hall, but towards the end Mr Southon had seemed to weary of visitors within minutes of their arrival and the Slades had thoughtfully stayed away, though they made regular telephone calls inquiring about the old man's health.

How, thought Kathryn on many occasions, did such a charming couple come to have a daughter like Delia? From the first she had liked them—and from the first she had disliked Delia—intensely. She had always adopted an imperious and condescending manner towards Kathryn, and there was a conceit about her that seemed quite obviously to stem from the fact that, being extraordinarily beautiful in every way, she attracted the admiring stares of both men and women alike. Perhaps I'm jealous, Kathryn thought. Perhaps I'm a horrid jealous little cat.

'I suggested we come on a visiting day,' Mrs Slade was saying, holding out her hand to Kathryn, who took it instantly, 'so as not to intrude on his privacy should he feel disinclined to receive callers.' She glanced vaguely around as if trying to pick out the new owner of Marbeck Hall from among the people strolling about. Failing in her efforts, she turned her attention again to Kathryn. 'How are you, dear? Is everything all right? He's settling here—at least for a while—from what we've heard, so I expect your job's all right. You were rather worried about it the last time we called.'

'I'm having to leave,' Kathryn informed them quietly. 'Mr Hyland doesn't require my services.'

'What a shame!' from Mr Slade, who looked genuinely distressed. 'You've been here since the place opened, haven't you? People are going to miss you, I'm sure.'

'I expect Kathryn will soon find herself another post,' Delia put in, and Kathryn instantly chided herself for mentally describing that half smile as a rather supercilious sneer.

'I expect I shall,' she agreed, though with a little inward sigh. Jobs there were in plenty these days . . . but not in such idyllic surroundings as this. She looked towards the Library, where John Hyland and Michael were still deep in conversation.

'Would you like me to take you to Mr Hyland?' she offered, and at once noticed the flickering light of interest which appeared in Delia Slade's lovely dark eyes. Faintly Kathryn's lips curved to a smile. Word had spread quickly that the new owner of Marbeck Hall was a remarkably handsome man. And remarkably handsome men were always of interest to Delia Slade. But she had reached the age of twenty-seven and was not yet married, though rumour had it she had turned down a great many offers. Kathryn could well believe this, and thought the reason must be that none of the would-be husbands were wealthy enough. Well, perhaps she and John Hyland would get together.

'If he isn't too busy,' Mr Slade was saying hesitantly. 'We'd very much like to meet him, but we don't want to interrupt anything.'

'He's talking to a visitor, but I'm sure he'll be pleased to meet you.' She led the way into the Library. John Hyland stopped talking and turned at her approach. Kathryn introduced them, noticing as she did so that Delia's interest was now deep and pronounced. Her dark eyes fluttered enchantingly; her lips parted in the sort of smile that only Delia could give, and a responsive smile came instantly to John Hyland's lips. He seemed to hold her hand longer than he need have done and for a moment he appeared to be oblivious of everyone else in the room except the lovely girl at his side. Kathryn explained that Mr and Mrs Slade had been old friends of Mr Southon and John's attention came at last from Delia to her parents. He smiled charmingly at them, expressing his pleasure at meeting them. But his manners were not lacking and as they all fell into casual conversation he made sure Michael was included. As the minutes passed, however, Kathryn realized that she herself was being left out, and with a murmured word of apology that no one appeared to notice, she slipped away to join several people who, though obviously interested in some china in a cabinet, did not know anything about it and were looking round for someone who could help them.

A little while later she was right at the top of the house, having just been explaining about the priest holes, and remarking on how cleverly they were hidden, when she heard Mrs Slade's voice on the landing below.

'I do love the view from this window. . . .'

So they were sauntering round. It was not unusual,
for Mr and Mrs Slade loved the house and in the old days
when they were regular visitors to the Hall they would
often stand and admire the view over to the heights of
the Derbyshire Pennines. After a while Kathryn came to
the lower floor, but the Slades and their host had disappeared and she presumed they had gone down to the
sitting-room. However, on passing her own room, she
was amazed to see the door marked 'Private' standing
wide open. Delia and her parents were in the room;
Delia was handling one of Kathryn's hairbrushes, and
just as a surge of anger brought the colour to her cheeks,
Kathryn sensed the presence of John Hyland behind her.

'This is Miss Ramsey's room,' he said. 'The door
was marked private, but perhaps you missed it.'

'Oh, I'm sorry,' murmured Delia, replacing the brush
on the tray. Then she smiled at Kathryn. 'What lovely
silver. You have excellent taste—and plenty of money,
by the looks of things.'

'They're Christmas and birthday presents from Mr
Southon,' Kathryn supplied, her colour deepening as
her anger increased. Delia Slade knew very well that this
was her room and, therefore, was never open to the
public.

'They look like part of a collection,' purred Delia, her
eyes on John while she spoke to Kathryn. 'Like family
heirlooms, in fact.'

'I believe they are part of a collection.' Kathryn
stood there, in an attitude of waiting, expecting them to
leave her room, but Delia did not intend taking the hint
as, still purring softly, she added,

'Mr Southon must have thought a great deal about
you.'

'He did,' remarked John suavely and, turning to
Kathryn, 'You enjoyed many privileges, didn't you,

Miss Ramsey?'

What did he mean? Convinced that his words hid a subtle insinuation, Kathryn walked stiffly past him and on to the landing, her temper almost out of control. How dared he make comments like that?—and in front of Delia Slade and her parents!

She was still fuming when, later in the afternoon, Burrows came to her as she was talking to some other visitors in the Gallery.

'Miss Ramsey,' he interrupted apologetically, 'Mr Hyland rang for one of the maids, but as you know it's Edna's day off and Emily's gone to bed with a cold.'

'It's all right, Burrows,' she said, after a slight hesitation. 'I'll go and see what Mr Hyland wants. Where is he?'

'In the sitting-room, with his visitors.'

John Hyland glanced up in surprise as she entered, and asked her to send Emily to him.

'She went to bed after lunch,' Kathryn informed him. 'She isn't at all well.'

'I see.' The merest pause and then, 'We require tea, Miss Ramsey; will you make it, please? Just something light, sandwiches and cakes—and quickly, because my visitors haven't much time.'

Kathryn hesitated, noticing the patronizing glance of Delia Slade and wondering whether or not to remind her employer that making afternoon tea was not part of her duties. But in the circumstances that would be churlish, for there was no one else to do it. Nevertheless, she felt that John Hyland could have used a rather more gracious approach, for he was after all requesting a favour.

She took the tea in on a silver tray, put it down on a table and turned to go.

'We'll have it over here.' John Hyland's voice was crisp; he seemed to know she was faintly annoyed at having to do this task. 'And I think we shall require more sandwiches.'

Kathryn flushed and left the room, returning ten minutes later with the sandwiches.

'Thank you.' He took the plate from her before she had time to put it on the table, and began to pass it round to his guests. Delia took one and, as she placed it on her plate she knocked her cake fork on to the floor.

'Oh—' She looked up at Kathryn, who was just moving away from the table. 'My fork. I'm so sorry.' She waited for Kathryn to stoop and pick it up, but Kathryn turned and would have left the room had not her employer called her back.

'Pick up Miss Slade's fork,' he said curtly, and almost choking with anger and mortification, Kathryn stooped and picked it up. 'Fetch a clean one,' said John Hyland without even waiting to see what Kathryn meant to do with it. She had fully intended fetching another, but the curt order only caused her to have more difficulty in suppressing her anger.

Delia Slade glanced up at her when she returned with the fork, and thanked her in a perfunctory manner, as though she were speaking to a servant.

Determined to put the unpleasant episode from her, Kathryn again mingled with the visitors, wandering about the rooms, and now and then going out to the garden. She was standing by the old well when John Hyland and the Slades came from the house. They were chatting and laughing together and Kathryn watched Delia for a moment as she used her charms to the full on the new owner of Marbeck Hall. No doubt, though, she was beautiful, Kathryn had to own. And she certainly knew how to use those enormous eyes. As if sensing the other girl's interest, Delia glanced over to where Kathryn was standing and, after a slight hesitation, left her parents and strolled across to her.

'I don't expect we shall see you again,' she drawled, all her charm appearing to have vanished on leaving her host, 'so I'll say goodbye. It must be an awful wrench for you after all this time, but as I said, you'll soon get another job—though perhaps not one where you'll have so much of your own way as you had with Mr Southon. He was a dear, the old man, but he really was rather soft with those who worked for him— Oh, perhaps I shouldn't have said that, but you know what I mean.'

'It's quite possible that Mr Southon got more out of his employees for being soft, as you call it. We all had a great affection for him, and would have done anything to please him.' Kathryn spoke quietly and with dignity; her manner seemed to annoy the other girl whose lovely eyes kindled for a moment, though her voice was pleasant when she spoke.

'He was certainly well liked. My mother and father miss him very much indeed.' She smiled and gestured towards the front door of the Hall, where her parents were in conversation with John Hyland. 'John is also going to be well liked, I'm sure. We were so pleasantly surprised on meeting him. I think he'll be more efficient, though, and certainly he'll never be so easy-going with the servants. He says himself that Mr Southon was far too lax.'

Lax with whom? With herself, no doubt, thought Kathryn, her anger rising again as she visualized John Hyland discussing her with this girl and her parents.

'People have their own methods,' she commented at last. 'No doubt Mr Hyland considers his will be an improvement on those of Mr Southon.'

'They're sure to be—he's so experienced in business methods, having so many interests in the United States.'

Had he said that? Kathryn wondered, frowning at the idea. No, much as she disliked him, she couldn't believe he would brag about his possessions. Delia had obviously been taking in all the newspapers had to say.

The other three were approaching and soon Mr and Mrs Slade were saying their goodbyes, and although there was genuine regret in their manner, their words were guarded.

This was natural, Kathryn owned, seeing that they were in the presence of the man who had dismissed her. Nevertheless, their attitude, usually so friendly and spontaneous, only added to the resentment she was beginning to feel against John Hyland. Hitherto she had accepted his decision as being fair. He didn't want her in his employ and had every right to tell her so. But he had no right to discuss her with these people, for he *had* discussed her, telling them, she supposed, about the reception he had been given on arrival, and probably mentioning the caravans, too, she thought, not without a feeling of guilt.

'Well, we really must go,' Mr Slade said, smiling as his daughter held out her hand to John Hyland. 'We'll see you tomorrow evening, then? We usually have dinner about eight, but come when you like, of course.'

'Come early,' urged Delia, casting him a fluttering glance from under her lashes. 'Then I can show you round our conservatories. Father was too modest just now; his orchids really are something special.'

CHAPTER III

Several circumstances contributed to Kathryn's changing her mind about meekly accepting John Hyland's dismissal and leaving his employ. Retaliation had first become the germ of an idea when he had said she enjoyed many privileges when employed by Mr Southon. This statement, she felt, could be interpreted as meaning she received favours from her late employer. Then, later, she had not only been put in the position of a servant, but had been made to feel one, deliberately, she believed, by John, and certainly by Delia. Nevertheless, these indignities in themselves would not have induced her to insist on John's observance of the provision made for her by Mr Southon, for in spite of them she still felt that John had a right to decide for himself whether or not he wanted to keep her in his employ. However, those slights did rankle, and when only two days before her intended departure she was severely reprimanded by her employer for using one of the cars, she told him, in the heat of the moment, that she was not leaving until the end of the year.

'I was using the car on estate business,' she flashed. 'There was a discrepancy in one of our—in one of the accounts, and as I couldn't convince the tradesman over the phone I decided to go into Macclesfield and take him proof of this mistake. I've always used the car and thought nothing of it.'

'You were in the habit of taking the car whenever you liked?—without asking or receiving permission from your employer?' he queried, raising his brows, and for the moment not particularly interested in her statement that she was not leaving until the end of the year.

'Mr Southon trusted me not to take advantage of his— his generosity. I could have a car whenever I wanted one, even for my own private use.'

'You were extremely fortunate, Miss Ramsey. I'm afraid I don't allow my employees such licence.' He paused before adding, curiously, 'What's this about your not leaving?'

Kathryn flushed and half wished she had not allowed her temper to get the better of her. However, the idea of staying had in fact been growing and she now explained about the clause in the will, wondering how it was he apparently knew nothing about it. The knowledge of its existence certainly took him by surprise, for he stared down at her in disbelief for a while before demanding a fuller explanation.

'Why wasn't I informed of this?' he asked wrathfully when she had finished. 'That solicitor fellow didn't mention it. Are you quite sure of your facts?' he added, eyeing her suspiciously.

'You can easily find out,' she replied, pale but now

quite determined to remain in her post. 'Mr Southon provided for me to stay on for a year after his death. I've almost five months left.'

He seemed puzzled, as he looked down at her from his great height, that metallic glint in his eyes seeming to bore into her.

'You gave me to understand you were leaving on Saturday. Why this sudden change of plan?'

Kathryn was standing just inside the door of the sitting-room, not having moved since he had sent for her immediately on her arrival back at the Hall from her visit to Macclesfield. John Hyland was standing in the centre of the room, immaculate in grey flannels and an expensive green linen jacket which had obviously been brought with him from the States. Kathryn felt somehow inadequate and with a little nervous movement she clasped her hands in front of her as if to gain some sort of confidence from the action. But her mouth felt strangely dry and she had difficulty in framing her words.

'I haven't another job to go to,' she began, when he interrupted her.

'That's not the reason for your change of plan.'

'No. . . .' Kathryn swallowed, thinking again of the type of man they had all expected, and how she herself had actually been prepared to adopt a faintly patronizing air with him. 'I don't think I have to give you a reason,' she managed at last, though she looked down at her hands, avoiding his gaze.

'I demand a reason, Miss Ramsey.' His tones were soft; indeed, Kathryn could not imagine his ever raising his voice, no matter how angry he might be. But that soft; indeed, Kathryn could not imagine his ever raising and Kathryn found herself saying,

'I feel you've not—not treated me with respect, or consideration, and—and—' She glanced up, flushing as she realized what this meant.

'You're staying on as an act of reprisal, as it were?'

He looked darkly at her, and she suspected his anger was beginning to smoulder beneath that cool exterior. ' This is your idea of retaliation? You'll stay on here even though you know I don't require your services?'

' It isn't retaliation, really. . . .'

' Come, Miss Ramsey, at least you can be honest.'

The ' at least ' filled her with indignation but she remained silent. By now she was fervently wishing she had taken his reprimand and left the room, for she felt herself to be in a most humiliating position. He waited a few moments, expecting some response, but eventually he said,

' The respect and consideration, as you term it, extended to you by your former employer seems to have been out of proportion. I certainly respect my employees —but I in turn wish for respect from them. I think you'll agree that the little scene I interrupted on my arrival here was far from respectful, and it amazes me that you thought for one moment that I'd keep you on.'

' That was most unfortunate, Mr Hyland, and I do apologize. Had I been more prudent, and not allowed my sisters to stay here, then it would never have happened. I really was upset about it.'

' You appeared to be enjoying it, nevertheless.'

There was no answer to that and Kathryn merely shrugged unhappily and lowered her eyes again. After a while he asked her if she were determined to remain at the Hall for another five months, and although Kathryn knew she should defer to his wishes, and leave, she seemed to be driven by some force stronger than herself as she said stubbornly,

' I'm staying, yes, Mr Hyland.'

There was a long moment of silence; John Hyland seemed to be deep in thought, but Kathryn also sensed his anger—and his frustration. He was helpless to do anything; Kathryn felt sure this was the first time in his life anyone had defied him and she also felt sure she would never be forgiven for putting him in this humiliating position. She ventured to glance up and a little quiver of apprehension passed through her as she caught again that dark metallic glint in his eyes.

'You realize your conduct is in complete defiance of my wishes, Miss Ramsey?' Kathryn said nothing, but stood there, biting her lip, and feeling that all the colour had by this time left her face. 'The situation will not be very comfortable for either of us, you do understand, I suppose?' His voice was a quiet threat, a very definite assurance that she would come to regret this obstinate disregard of his wishes. She said unsteadily,

'I suppose, in the circumstances, the situation will be awkward, but—' she glanced at him with a firm resolve in her eyes—' I intend to take advantage of the provision which Mr Southon made for me.'

As the days passed Kathryn began more and more to regret her decision to remain at the Hall, for, as she had suspected her life was being made as unpleasant as possible by her employer. He asked her to do things which he knew very well were not included in her duties, and she suspected he was waiting for her to raise some objections. He would then be within his rights to complain about her conduct and have a legitimate excuse for refusing to pay her salary, in which case she would have no alternative but to leave of her own accord. However, Kathryn steadfastly obeyed all his commands and orders, even though at times it went very much against the grain and she would then have the greatest difficulty in controlling her temper.

One occasion was particularly trying and she thought the time had actually come when she would be driven to handing in her notice. John had invited the Slades and their daughter to dinner. Emily, who was again unwell, had gone home to be cared for by her mother, and as this left only Edna to do both the cooking and waiting at

51

table, Kathryn gave her a helping hand. They were both in the kitchen when John came in and spoke to Kathryn, in the frigid tones he always used to her, whether they were alone or in the company of others.

'You'll wait on the table, Miss Ramsey. I want dinner served at eight-thirty.'

'I've arranged to go out this evening,' she returned. 'I'll help Edna all I can and see that everything's ready. She says she can then manage very well on her own.' Kathryn had been washing fruit; she was now drying it and putting it into a silver bowl. 'I always go out on Thursdays—'

'You always used to go out on Thursdays,' he interrupted haughtily, adding, 'And just whenever you liked, it seems to me. But this evening I shall expect you to be in and, as I've said, you'll wait at table.'

Kathryn cast a swift glance at Edna, who was staring in some surprise, waiting for Kathryn's reaction, and, no doubt, thinking this was very different from the way Kathryn was treated by Mr Southon.

'I've made a date, with Mr Robson—you met him just after you came, if you remember. He talked to you about the pictures.' Her voice was low, but vibrant with indignation at his treatment of her before Edna. Always the servants had looked up to Kathryn, regarding her rather in the light of a mistress. She had enjoyed the prestige while at the same time not in any way exploiting it at the servants' expense. In fact, the relationship between everyone in the household had been pleasant, far more pleasant than it was since the coming of the new owner to the Hall.

'Then I'm afraid you must phone Mr Robson and tell him you're unable to keep the date. I require your services this evening, Miss Ramsey, and I expect my wishes to be obeyed.' And with that he left her staring after him as he strode along the wide corridor separating the kitchens from the rest of the house. Her face burned as she resumed her task, and she avoided Edna's eyes. What should she do? John Hyland was waiting for her deliberate defiance, waiting for an excuse to stop her salary. She should never have insisted on staying here in the first place, Kathryn told herself, not for the first time, for never in her life had she felt so utterly miserable. It was incredible that she could be so unhappy at the Hall, the place she loved as if it were her own. A deep sigh escaped her, a sigh of regret for the happy years that were gone, the years when she had been treated with kindness and respect by her employer. Why did things have to change like this?

She telephoned Michael, explaining that they had a maid off work ill and she, Kathryn, would therefore have to help with the dinner. He was keenly disappointed, but they made another date for the following evening. This satisfied Michael and after laughingly telling her he was throwing her a kiss over the phone, he said good night and rang off. He was nice, thought Kathryn, realizing that her friendship with Michael was one of the few bright spots in her life nowadays. But she also looked forward to seeing her parents, whom she visited once a week. Also, she visited Mrs Percival occasionally, and one or two of the other old people whom she had befriended—much to her cost.

Delia Slade looked ravishing in a cocktail dress of silver lamé, with a magnificent necklace of diamonds round her throat and a diamond stud in her hair. Kathryn wore a plain blue cotton dress and her hair was tied back with a ribbon so as not to fall on to her shoulders when she leant over the guests, serving the food. Never before had she done such a menial task, but somehow she performed it with dignity, and despite the obvious satisfaction of Delia, she retained a calm front and even managed to smile at the Slades and answer pleasantly when they spoke to her. But their manner was cool, so very different from their previous attitude of friendliness and their way of treating Kathryn as an equal.

The meal over, she was asked by John to bring the coffee into the sitting-room and when she arrived with it Delia and John were standing very close together examining a lovely Landseer—*The Return from Hawking*.

' It's the colours, John, they're so marvellous!' Delia slid a hand along the bottom of the gilt frame, an elegant hand which then came to rest—quite by accident, it seemed, so cleverly was it done—on John's arm, which was also outstretched as he pointed to something in the painting. They then both stood away, to view the picture from a distance. Delia's hand still rested on his arm and he looked down, smiling at her. She returned his smile and despite her dislike of the girl Kathryn found herself catching her breath in admiration. She would captivate John Hyland, she must, for she was devastatingly beautiful. And he was extraordinarily good-looking too; in fact they made a most handsome pair, a couple who would most certainly attract attention wherever they went. Kathryn's glance moved to Mr Slade, and then to his wife; both were watching their daughter, and a look of satisfaction had settled on their faces.

' Oh, thank you, Kathryn,' said Mrs Slade graciously yet coolly as Kathryn served her coffee. ' Just leave Delia's and John's—they'll pour their own when they're ready.'

Later, as she lay on the lovely French bed, her eyes staring unseeingly at the carvings, Kathryn wondered whether to hand in her notice on the following morning. She was reluctant to accept defeat, but on the other hand she could not tolerate another evening such as this one had been. John's arrogance, Delia's supercilious and condescending attitude, and her parents' cool politeness of manner; these she had endured with apparent calm, but not without rancour. The next morning, however, she was surprised by the hint of a change in her employer's attitude towards her.

54

She had typed some letters and taken them in for him to sign. As she turned to go 'he called her back and asked if she knew of a contractor who would take on the work of filling a pond which was completely dry.

'From these old records I find that this depression was a small lake at one time,' he said, tapping some papers lying on his desk. 'I think I'd like to have it filled again.'

Kathryn did not reply at once, so great was her surprise, for not once had her new employer discussed things with her, or taken her into his confidence as had been the way with his predecessor.

'That was a fifth lake at one time,' she said at length, 'but Mr Southon tried to fill it and failed. It's something to do with the underlying rocks; the water drains away almost as quickly as it's put in.'

John frowned and queried this, pointing out, quite reasonably, that the rock structure could hardly change in such a small distance.

'The other four lakes are so close. No—' he shook his head, 'I'm sure it can be filled.'

'It'll be an expense for nothing,' Kathryn persisted, even though she was reluctant to argue with him. 'Mr Southon did persevere, but they just can't keep the water in.'

'I'll try, nevertheless. Do you know of a contractor who will do the work?'

She knew of two, and found him the addresses.

'Mr Southon had estimates from both, and it was this one who took the work on,' she said, handing him the paper on which she had written the information he required.

Later that day Delia called, driving her sports car right up to the front door of the Hall. Kathryn answered her ring; Delia smiled in her usual superior manner and asked for John.

'He's somewhere in the grounds,' Kathryn said, trying not to show her dislike of this girl. 'He won't be long—if you'd care to wait.' She took her into the sitting-room and, feeling it would be rude to leave her, she sat down, though she did wonder what they would have to say to one another. They had never had anything in common, but at one time they could converse fairly amicably. Since John Hyland's coming, however, Delia had for some reason become far more patronizing in her manner towards her, and Kathryn suspected the reason was that her own status had fallen considerably since Mr Southon's death. Seating herself on the couch, Delia broached the subject of Kathryn's former dismissal for the first time as she said, casting her a sideways glance,

'You gave us to understand John didn't want you. What happened that you're still here? Mother and Father are rather puzzled about it, but they didn't like to question you.'

But you would, thought Kathryn, at the same time chiding herself for always seizing on any opportunity of putting Delia in a bad light. And because she felt rather guilty she answered her question, speaking with much more cordiality than she felt.

'Mr Southon made provision for me to stay on until the end of the year,' she explained, 'so I decided to take advantage of that.'

'But you had at first intended leaving. We said good-bye to you.'

'I changed my mind,' was all that Kathryn would say to that, but the other girl did not intend letting the subject drop yet.

'Wasn't John annoyed? I mean, he said he didn't need you—or so you told us.'

'The matter was out of his hands,' replied Kathryn stiffly, no longer making an effort at politeness. 'I had a right to stay and I asserted my right.'

Delia leant back on the couch and crossed one elegant

leg over the other. Her eyes were fixed on Kathryn for a space before they began to flicker and then her long lashes came down, hiding her expression.

'John wouldn't like that—having you telling him what to do, as it were.'

'I have never told him what to do!'

'Isn't asserting your right, as you call it, telling him what he must do?'

'I don't think so. I would never presume to tell Mr Hyland what he must do.'

'Nevertheless, he must have been very annoyed at finding he couldn't dismiss you. After all, the place is his now and he'd naturally want to run it in his own particular way.'

'He does run it in his own way,' responded Kathryn coldly. 'My staying here doesn't interefere with his methods—how could it?'

Delia shrugged, and before Kathryn could reply to that John entered, a smile of welcome softening his face as his eyes lighted on his visitor.

'I hope you didn't mind my dropping in,' she smiled, using her lashes as she glanced up at him. 'I'd been shopping and thought I'd come back this way and call on you for half an hour or so.'

'Mind?—certainly not. I'm delighted to see you.' He paused as Kathryn rose and made to leave the room. Then he spoke to her, telling her he had rung the contractor, who was coming to make another attempt at filling the lake. His manner was again less frigid and his eyes less hard. Kathryn smiled at him and said she hoped he would be more successful than Mr Southon had been when he endeavoured to have the lake filled.

'I hope so,' he returned, and Kathryn could not be quite sure, but the merest flicker of a smile seemed to touch his mouth in response to the smile still lingering on her own lips. What she *was* sure of was the sudden narrowing of Delia's eyes as she glanced from Kathryn to John and then back to Kathryn again. Her mouth was tight, too, but as John turned to give her his attention her lips parted softly and her lovely eyes widened as they looked up to meet his admiring gaze. Kathryn left the room, quite sure that neither had even noticed her departure.

Michael came for her at seven; John happened to be at the front as he pulled up and he immediately went over to him, greeting him affably and inviting him in to wait for Kathryn. She came down almost at once, looking most attractive in a flowered linen dress, sleeveless and short. She carried a white handbag and gloves, and her hair was held in place with a matching white headband.

'Gosh, you look sweet!' exclaimed Michael, forgetting John's presence for a second as he turned to watch Kathryn as she came through the great dining-room into the hall. 'Doesn't she, Mr Hyland?'

A deep flush rose to tint Kathryn's cheeks and she felt almost cross with Michael. John Hyland would not be pleased at having to comment on her appearance. But he ignored the question, although his eyes did flicker over her, as if he saw her for the very first time. His silence impressed itself on Michael who, realizing his lack of tact, flushed slightly and said, in an effort to throw off his embarrassment,

'Shall we go?'

Kathryn smiled and nodded; they both said 'good evening' to John and then went out to the car.

'What's he like to work for?' Michael wanted to know as they drove alongside the lake before turning off on to the lane leading to the main road. 'He's great to talk to, but—well, he seems rather impersonal when he's with you. Is he as good a boss as Mr Southon?'

Kathryn shook her head, and went on to explain about his wanting her to go.

'I intended to at first,' she continued, her eyes on the

pretty, tree-lined lane ahead. 'But he was so horrid to me that I decided to stay on.'

'To spite him, eh?' he grinned. 'But the atmosphere won't be at all pleasant, will it, in the circumstances?'

'It isn't, but we manage to get along without any open animosity.'

'What will you do when you leave?' He turned on to the main road and increased his speed. 'You won't get another job of that sort. What did you do before going to the Hall?'

'I went there straight from school,' she replied wistfully, recalling that wonderful day when she had sped home on winged feet to tell her mother she was going to work at Marbeck Hall. And now it was all over—or almost so. Another four months and she would leave it for ever. She could come back as a visitor, of course, but Kathryn knew she would never do that. Once she left, with her belongings, it would be for the last time; she would never enter the Hall again. 'I don't know what I shall do—go into an office, I expect,' she added dejectedly.

They went to a cinema in Macclesfield, then called at a roadhouse on the way home and had a meal. It was almost midnight when at last they reached the Hall, for Michael had drawn into a farm gateway and they had sat talking for over an hour, mainly about antiques. Michael was going abroad in two weeks' time, and was hoping to have some new and interesting items for his shop when he returned.

'I wish you could come with me,' he said as they were once more on the road. 'It isn't possible, I suppose? Have you had your holidays yet?'

'I usually take them in the autumn, when we've finished with the visitors. In any case, it wouldn't be right for me to go abroad with you, Michael.'

'Why not? We'd have two rooms with two views. I'm not a bit like that.' He laughed and Kathryn joined in. 'Will you come, if I wait?' She shook her head.

'I won't say I wouldn't like to come with you, but what would people say?'

They had reached the drive; he proceeded slowly between two beautiful lakes and pulled up at the front door. Lights were shining from the side windows of the sitting-room.

'If one worried about gossip, Kathryn,' he said, taking her hand and holding it gently, 'one would never do anything or go anywhere. I make it a rule never to bother my head with what other people think.'

'An excellent idea, if you can do it,' she agreed, deriving an odd sort of comfort from his hold on her hand. 'But I'm afraid I can't, so don't change your plans because of me.'

The night was warm and sultry and when Michael had driven away Kathryn stood for a while on the step, looking up at the stars and then across to the largest lake where the reflection of the crescent moon floated among the reeds and water-lilies. She heard the sound coming from the side of the house, the soft but firm tread of John Hyland; then he too was on the step, standing beside her, so tall and straight, his brown hair tousled slightly, making him appear more human than Kathryn had ever seen him.

'It's a very beautiful night,' he said, surprising her, both by the appreciative note in his voice and by the way he looked down at her and smiled. 'I've been out walking; the air here's wonderful.'

'We're very close to the Derbyshire moors,' she informed him. 'And the air there is really invigorating. It blows over to us at times.'

'Derbyshire . . . ? Very bleak in winter, so I'm told.'

'The moors are, yes. But not at this time of the year. The heather's out now and the bracken's turning. The colours are really beautiful.' She paused shyly before she added, 'You should go up there—have a day. I'm sure you'd thoroughly enjoy it.'

'I believe I should.' His tones were soft and lazy; Kathryn was used to that drawl by now, but always she found something extremely attractive in it. Tonight, to her puzzlement and surprise, it seemed to affect her profoundly; she could not explain her emotions, but she was conscious of groping vaguely for some elusive thing and, unable to discover it, was left with a feeling of emptiness and even loss.

It must be something to do with leaving the Hall, she concluded, but even as John moved, almost brushing against her unconsciously as he half turned to glance away towards the high tower of the church, Kathryn felt a strange quickening of her pulse; again the sensation was vague, and yet disturbing because of its very lack of substance.

And she was unsure of herself too, which was not like her at all, for one of the assets contributing to the success of her job was that of confidence. But talking to the visitors was very different from talking to John Hyland. He was far too superior; he possessed a certain arrogance made none the less disconcerting because of its presence beneath the surface. His whole bearing was one of the aristocrat, and once again Kathryn reflected on what the newspapers had written about the new heir, the cowboy from the Rockies who would never have the slightest notion how to go on in one of England's most famous stately homes.

What would their relationship have been had he not made such an untimely appearance? Kathryn wondered. Had she been prepared, had she come up to his expectations, been the sort of person described to him by Mr Lowry, then everything would have been so different. Kathryn felt sure he would not have dismissed her. She gave a little sigh. What use now to dwell on what might have been? Through her own folly and thoughtlessness she had antagonized him; his pride must have suffered greatly as he stood there, watching the skit on himself, and Kathryn was very sure he would never forgive her for that humiliation.

'I think I must go in,' she remarked, finding difficulty in speaking at all. But the silence was becoming oppressive and she herself felt awkward and, somehow, in the way.

'Yes, it's quite late.' He stood aside for Kathryn to enter first, and then locked and bolted the door behind him. He seemed almost too tall for the room, Kathryn thought as he straightened up. For the ceiling was very low and beamed and he appeared to be a giant beside the suit of armour displayed against the wall at one side of the door. The Library was to the right and as his eyes strayed to the open door he seemed to hesitate, undecided. Then he said quietly, 'Before you leave, Miss Ramsey, I would like you to give me some account of the books here. I see there is a large section on Cheshire, and I would like to have your advice on which to read, because I must know more about this place where I now live. You know which are the best books, I suppose?'

His question surprised her, for she never expected him to ask her advice.

'I do know the best books, yes,' she murmured. 'I'll make a list for you.'

'No, we can spend some time in there; I want to know exactly what I have and I don't think there's any reason for waiting. Perhaps on Tuesday, after the rush of the week-end, and when the accounts are all done,' he decided. 'Yes, we'll make it Tuesday.' The glimmer of a smile curved his mouth as he bade her good night before striding away, leaving her to stare after him, her mind in a turmoil as she tried to grasp the fact that, for the very first time, he had adopted a civil—and almost friendly—manner towards her.

For the first time he had not made her acutely conscious of the strain she felt in his presence, the strain resulting from the memory of that first disastrous meeting between them.

At last she moved and went upstairs, entering the Blue Room, and mentally trying to count the number of nights left to her in this beautiful and elegant apartment. Kings and princes had slept in the Hall Room, she knew, but what famous people had slept here? She stood in the centre of the room, dwelling for a while on the splendour of those medieval days when the house was at the height of its glory, musing on that age of chivalry when great banquets were held in honour of royal guests, when buck shooting took place in the grounds and colourful pageantry was displayed when the tournaments were fought out on the tilting ground in the park.

When at last Kathryn undressed and slipped into bed she dozed and wakened on and off for a long while, and in her half-sleep she saw herself living in those far-off days, and she saw John Hyland ordering the most hideous tortures to be inflicted on her in reprisal for the insult he had received on first coming to the Hall.

CHAPTER IV

September colours were tinting the countryside; the weather had changed, too, bringing a nip into the morning air, and Kathryn had a fire lighted in the Library both to supplement the central heating and also to add to the cheerfulness of the room.

John had said they would spend the afternoon on the books, and as a breeze was blowing rather hard Kathryn went upstairs to close her bedroom window. As she came into the Gallery she heard a faint sound and went to investigate. In the Solar bedroom she found her employer, moving around and sniffing audibly. He glanced up as she stood in the doorway, and asked her if she could smell anything.

'I know it's ridiculous,' he drawled, 'but I'll swear I can smell incense.' He looked at her challengingly, as if expecting her to laugh, but at the same time daring her to do so.

'Yes, I can smell it,' she smiled, faintly amused by his puzzlement. 'We aren't— The house isn't actually haunted, but this smell is sometimes here, in the Solar Room.' A tiny laugh did break from her lips now, for despite his challenge, he looked a trifle taken aback by her admission.

'There's some explanation for it?' He stood by the bed, casting a frowning glance around the timbered walls.

Kathryn nodded, and walked further into the room.

'We think it comes from the room almost directly below this,' she told him, and his brow furrowed in thought.

'The smaller hall's below this, I believe?'

'The one leading into the courtyard, yes.'

'And what happened there? Was some particularly foul murder committed?' He seemed faintly amused and smilingly awaited her explanation.

'About fifty years ago a skeleton was found in an old cupboard—' She broke off as his smile turned to laughter.

'A skeleton in a cupboard?—really?'

'It was when they were removing the cupboard,' Kathryn corrected, 'and it was found behind, in the wall. No one has ever discovered anything about it—but I expect it was a murder. They buried the bones in the churchyard.'

'A murder mystery. . . . Well, I suppose every English stately home worth its salt has a ghost, or a mystery of some sort.' No doubting his amusement, and Kathryn could not curb the hint of breathlessness she experienced at the change in his stern and forbidding countenance. And she could not understand that breath-

64

lessness either, for it remained with her long after they had left the Solar Room to go downstairs to the small hall from which it was thought the smell of incense emanated.

'This is where the cupboard was.' Kathryn showed him the wall, so innocent-looking with all the scars of the alteration erased.

'What was this room—in the old days?' he asked, glancing round with a new interest.

'In medieval times it was the steward's office. In those days there was the Manorial Court, which was held periodically—but you know about that.'

'I don't know a lot about those things,' he admitted, surprisingly. 'I gather the function of the court was to deal with problems concerning the Manor, though?'

'Yes; there were all sorts of differences occurring between the peasants, and these would be brought before the court. Also, the peasants could be tried for offences against each other, and for disobeying the rules of the Manor—and for offences against the lord himself, of course.'

At that he turned slowly round, looking at her long and hard, but no comment was forthcoming and a short while later they were in the Library, methodically going through the books, shelf by shelf. Both were so engrossed that the time flew and with a little gasp Kathryn realized it was long past their tea time.

'I think it can be brought in here,' John decided, ringing the bell. 'There's much I still want to know. We haven't even finished these shelves here yet. This is going to take much longer than I anticipated.'

'Do you want me to have mine in here?' she asked, unable to hide her surprise when John gave Edna the order to fetch the tea into the Library.

'I don't see why not.' His interest was with the book he held and his words came automatically; nevertheless, they had the most odd effect on Kathryn's composure.

Why should she suddenly feel like this? Was she being so foolish as to think he would forget the slight he had received?—would overlook her several offences which must have appeared so presumptuous to him at the time? Did she cherish the hope that he might decide to keep her on? No doubt about the answer to those questions; from the beginning she had hoped that by some miracle he would come to change his mind.

They sat at the small table by the fire, eating sandwiches and cakes, and talking about books. John was keenly interested and when tea was over Kathryn resumed her task of increasing her employer's knowledge of the lovely treasures that had come so unexpectedly into his possession.

' I think we'll leave it for today,' he said at length, glancing at the clock. ' It's only just over an hour to dinner and I've invited the Slades.'

Several books lay about and Kathryn returned them to the shelves, her pleasure evaporating at his words. The afternoon had been the happiest since the coming of John Hyland. For the first time they had worked together in harmony; she had forgotten the friction that existed between them—and she felt sure that he had forgotten it, too, if only for a short while. Why the coming of the Slades should have this sudden adverse effect on her spirits she could not say—unless it was because of her intense dislike of their daughter.

For a couple of weeks after spending those two pleasant days in the Library with John Kathryn felt inexplicably restless and flat. On trying to discover a reason for this the only conclusion reached was that, as her employer had thawed no further in his attitude towards her, her own position was in no way changed. She was to leave, it seemed, at the end of the year.

But towards the middle of September John again surprised her by dropping his cool indifference as he said, with a faint grimace, accompanied by a shrug of resignation,

'You were right about the lake, Miss Ramsey. As you know, work has been going on for some time, but the contractors have given it up. It's as you said, something to do with the underlying rocks; they're more permeable than the rest of the rocks around here.'

Kathryn was cleaning silver—the magnificent candelabra from the Dining-Room—and she glanced up from her task, surprised by his admission, and by the smile appearing on his face.

'It's a pity,' she returned, vaguely wondering what the experiment had cost him, for the men had been working down at the lake for weeks. 'But I don't think it's all that important. We have four lakes and they're all very beautiful.' Unaware of the wistful note in her voice, Kathryn was puzzled by the odd expression that came to her employer's face.

'You're extremely attached to this house, aren't you?' he said, glancing from the duster in her hand to the ornate piece of silver on the table.

Faintly startled, Kathryn wondered if he had noticed her use of the word 'we' again, and she hesitated uncertainly before answering,

'One can't help but become attached to it, Mr Hyland.'

'You've been here six years, so you told me?'

She nodded, reflecting on Mr Lowry's praise for the way she had managed since Mr Southon's death. He had said he could do nothing else but recommend her highly to the new owner of the Hall. John Hyland had naturally been puzzled at finding her so different from what he expected; perhaps he had been puzzled since, for despite his attitude towards her she had continued to work efficiently and conscientiously, having his interests at heart even though she was soon to be leaving his employ.

'I came to Mr Southon when I was seventeen,' she said, as he stood there in silence apparently expecting an answer.

'So this was your first job?'

'Yes.' Her eyes searched his face; there was a new interest here, and a certain friendliness he had not displayed since those days in the Library when they had worked together on the books. 'I came as the guide, when the Hall was first opened to the public.'

'And then you gradually took on all these extra duties . . . which meant your living at the Hall.' He was murmuring to himself, or so it seemed, and Kathryn recalled his saying that she had made herself almost indispensable to Mr Southon.

'It was owing to his health, and the extra duties were taken on gradually.' Her gaze was unhappy as she continued, 'Mr Southon relied on me, and I wouldn't have dreamed of letting him down.' He did not reply immediately; when he did Kathryn felt certain she detected a hint of regret as he said,

'I'm sure you wouldn't, Miss Ramsey. You must have been a great help to your former employer.'

From then on life for Kathryn became more pleasant; she was now consulted on matters which were not clear to John, and her hopes of retaining her post had risen when on the following Sunday, after the doors had closed on the last of the visitors, he had said,

'What exactly did you do during the winter months, Miss Ramsey?'

'During the time the house was closed? I didn't have as much to do then, but I cleaned all the silver and washed the china.' She smiled faintly and added, 'You have a great deal of that, and Mr Southon would never trust it to either of the maids. Then there were always some letters, and other paper work. And later, as I mentioned, I drove Mr Southon about—until he was unable to go out, that was.'

'I see.' He mused on this for a while and Kathryn waited, with faint expectancy, hoping he would add to it. But if the idea of retaining her services had occurred to him he had no intention of informing her about it yet awhile.

By the middle of October the crowds visiting the Hall had dwindled, but not appreciably so, for although the morning air was crisp and cold the afternoons were warm and sunny and there were prospects of an Indian summer. Delia was now a regular visitor to the Hall, and Kathryn suspected John was a regular, and welcome, visitor to the Slades'. And then one afternoon when Michael took Kathryn out for a run in his car he casually remarked,

' There's talk of an engagement between your boss and Delia Slade—but of course you must have heard?'

She shook her head.

' I haven't heard, no, but they've become very friendly this last month or so.'

' More than friendly; they've had their pictures in the local rag several times lately. They're going about together, that's for sure.' He drew on to the forecourt of a little black and white building and brought the car to a standstill. ' Tea for two—okay?'

She smiled. Invariably they stopped at the Tudor for afternoon tea.'

' Okay,' she returned, and got out of the car.

The waitress gave them a corner table, facing the garden. Flowers were still in bloom and the sun was shining down from a clear blue sky. Michael sat close to her and Kathryn tried to edge away without making it apparent that she was doing so. No doubt in her mind that Michael was becoming serious, but Kathryn's thoughts were elsewhere. Would her employer marry Delia? Strange that at first she had viewed the possibility without any sort of emotion whatsoever . . . but now. . . . Now she felt a peculiar little nagging pain inside her at the idea of Delia's becoming John Hyland's wife. Yet she had to admit they were admirably suited, belonging as they did to the same set. Their natures, too, appeared to be in harmony, for both possessed an air of superiority, and an underlying arrogance that gave the impression of coldness. That this coldness existed in Delia's make-up Kathryn did not for one moment doubt, but with John she was not so sure. For lately she had seen a quite different side to his nature, a side which seemed to convince her he was not nearly so cold and unfeeling as his haughty exterior would imply.

'What are you having?' Michael's low and pleasant voice cut into her thoughts and she turned to give him a smile.

'The usual.' Kathryn glanced up at the waitress. 'Home-made scones?'

The waitress nodded.

'And jam and cream?'

'Cakes, too,' added Michael. 'But a pot of tea first, if you please.'

They were the only occupants of the café, and Kathryn found herself in an intimate situation which she would have given much to avoid.

Michael said thoughtfully,

'You'll be leaving in about ten weeks or so?'

'Yes, that's right.' Dejection flooded over her, for John had still made no mention of keeping her on at the Hall. 'I suppose I ought to begin looking round for another job.'

Michael glanced up and waited until the tray had been placed on the table.

'How would you like to work in the shop with me?'

Kathryn turned her head in surprise.

'In antiques? I'd love it, but you don't require an assistant.'

'I wasn't thinking of an assistant, as such.' His hand covered hers as it lay idly on the table. 'How about you and me getting married? We've got the same interests and I'm sure we'd get along fine,' and he added, with a little laugh, 'I love you, Kathryn, truly. I

70

suppose I should have said that first.

'I—I—' Hastily Kathryn withdrew her hand and picked up the cream jug. 'I can't marry you, Michael,' she said, an unconscious note of apology in her voice. 'I don't love you—I mean, I've never thought of marriage, not to anyone.'

'Naturally you don't think of marriage until you meet someone,' he returned reasonably, not too put out by her refusal. 'For the past six years you've been completely wrapped up in your job; you've said yourself you never had much time to get out and meet people. Well, you've met someone now, and I know you like me, otherwise you'd never have come out with me in the first place. You're not that kind of a girl.'

'I do like you,' she said seriously, 'but that isn't love.' She poured the milk into the cups, keeping her head averted to hide the confusion on her face. 'I can't marry you, Michael. Please don't let's talk about it any more.'

'But you haven't a job, and it's going to be difficult finding one you'll really like.'

She smiled faintly.

'That's no reason for getting married,' she said, pouring his tea. 'In any case, I'll get a job without any trouble.'

'Not one you'll be happy in, though.'

'I might. I haven't looked around, have I?'

He shrugged, slightly downcast, but by no means defeated.

'I meant it when I said I loved you, Kathryn. And I feel sure you could love me, if you tried.'

If she tried. One did not have to try when it came to loving. It just happened.

'Please let it drop,' she begged, passing him his tea. 'I don't want to be married. I'm quite happy as I am.'

'You can't go on like this for ever, though. All girls want to get married.' Kathryn heaved a deep sigh and asked him once again to let the matter drop. 'All right —but only for now. I'll ask you again, when I've decided you've had time to think it over.'

Dusk was falling when they arrived back at the Hall, and John was standing on the step, gazing out across to the dark outline of the distant hills. He invited Michael in for a drink and they all went to the sitting-room, Michael and John soon becoming engaged in their favourite topic, paintings. Kathryn listened, speaking only when spoken to, but for some reason feeling strangely content and happy. Why this new sensation? There was no accounting for it, and yet it remained. Remained, that is, until, on answering the front door bell, Kathryn came face to face with Delia Slade.

'Is John in?' Delia swept past Kathryn without waiting for an answer. She looked young and chic in a tailored dress of fine tweed, its only ornamentation being a diamond and pearl brooch pinned to one corner of the high collar. Her hair was attractively styled without appearing too immaculate, and the merest hint of perfume emanated from somewhere about her person. She must captivate him, Kathryn thought, closing the door behind her. It was impossible that he could resist anyone so devastatingly beautiful.

'We're all in the sitting-room,' she said, turning to lead the way.

'All?' The tones were crisp and cold, and there was a haughty lift of Delia's brows.

'Michael and I are with Mr Hyland.' Kathryn said no more, and she did not give Delia time to say more either, as she hurried away in the direction of the room in which the two men were still deeply engaged in conversation.

'Delia—how nice!' John rose instantly and drew out a chair for her. 'You've met Mr Robson?' and, when Delia nodded and smiled charmingly at Michael, 'Can I get you a drink?'

'Thank you, John.' Her long lashes fluttered as she looked up at him, and her lips were still parted in a smile. 'I hope I'm not intruding,' she added, her glance moving swiftly over the two other occupants of the room.

'You're never intruding,' said John on a faintly admonishing note. 'You should know by now that you're always welcome here.'

Delia took the drink, her gaze meeting that of Kathryn, who was staring intently at her. For a moment John had his back to Delia as he moved over to his chair, and the smile on her lips vanished momentarily as Delia's expression took on the light of triumph. After holding her gaze for a space Kathryn glanced away; at the same time John sat down and the smile swiftly returned to Delia's lips. For a while Delia kept all John's attention, but then he and Michael began to discuss pictures again. A slight disagreement arose and presently both got up and, with a word of apology to the girls, they left them, with the intention of going to the Gallery in order to examine the painting under discussion and thereby settle the argument.

A small silence followed their departure, and then Delia looked across at Kathryn, and the smile became the usual supercilious curve that was invariably in evidence on those occasions when Delia found herself alone with Kathryn.

'You and John seem to have resolved your differences,' she purred, leaning forward to take her glass from the table beside her.

'Differences?'

'He wasn't pleased at the idea of your staying on here after he'd told you to go, but he seems to have forgotten it now. I'm glad,' she added, obviously realizing just how tactless she was being. 'It must have been unpleasant for both of you.'

Kathryn hesitated.

'Did Mr Hyland tell you he wasn't pleased at my

remaining here?' She had to ask the question, although she found difficulty in doing so.

Delia's lids drooped.

'Not in so many words, but it was plain that he was dreadfully annoyed.' A pause and then, silkily, 'I can understand your attitude, in a way, because you had no other work to go to, but I'm afraid I couldn't have gone against John's wishes like that. He's bound to be harbouring some sort of resentment against you.'

Kathryn sank back in her chair, crossing her legs and staring straight at the other girl with undisguised disdain.

'I don't see why he should harbour resentment against me, Delia. It was Mr Southon's wish that I should stay on for a year after his death—and it's not unusual for the provisions made in a will to be observed, just the contrary, in fact.'

'Oh, I agree, to a certain extent. But from John's point of view the provision must have seemed irksome.'

'I don't see that he has any complaint,' came the tart rejoinder. 'Mr Hyland was lucky to have inherited this place at all. It was only because Mr Southon never married, and because there were no nearer relatives. Mr Hyland's claim to the estate was extremely flimsy.' Kathryn had been impelled to hit back, but she regretted her words immediately they were uttered, for she was sure they gave the impression that she resented John Hyland's inheriting the estate.

A slow smile came to Delia's mouth; she sipped her wine thoughtfully. There was an odd hint of satisfaction in her manner which, for some reason, sent a quiver of apprehension down Kathryn's spine. But she shook it off, annoyed with herself for allowing Delia to affect her in this way. They sat in silence for a while and then, to Kathryn's relief, the two men returned. Delia flashed John a smile and asked if the argument was settled.

'Yes.' It was Michael who spoke, ruefully. 'Mr

Hyland was right. I don't know why I argued, because I suspected he would know more than I.'

A generous admission, thought Kathryn, for Michael was himself extremely knowledgeable about paintings.

'I'm sure I don't know more than you,' said John graciously, sitting down on the couch opposite to Kathryn. 'I have a great respect for your judgement; it was only that in this particular case I felt I was right because I happen to have some Reynolds at home.' Kathryn lifted her head quickly and he added, 'In the United States, I should have said. This is my home now.'

'You're quite settled?' Michael asked, watching John with interest. 'You've no yearnings to go back?'

'Obviously I have yearnings; but it's my intention to settle here.' By accident or design his eyes met Delia's, and his expression became thoughtful. Then he glanced at Kathryn. She caught her breath; that odd feeling of restlessness crept over her and she could not take her eyes off his face. He smiled faintly, and Kathryn instantly became aware of Delia watching them. Turning, Kathryn gave a little start of surprise—for there was no mistaking the look of enmity on the older girl's face. But even as she tried to discover some reason for it Delia's expression underwent a swift and dramatic change as John's eyes rested on her. An enchanting smile flashed in his direction and he quickly responded, quite unaware of the hostility that smile had just replaced.

But Kathryn remained acutely conscious of that hostility, and she was glad when Michael at last rose and said he must be going. She rose also and prepared to leave the room along with him.

'A man wants to consult me about a porcelain group he's bought. He's wondering if it could be Meissen.' Michael smiled a little sceptically. 'I shouldn't think it is, not judging by the price he's paid, but you never know. There are still bargains to be had if one happens

75

to be lucky.'

'Meissen would be marked,' asserted Delia with some authority, but instinctively Kathryn shook her head.

'Early Meissen wasn't marked,' she said, and Delia threw her another glance of animosity as John nodded in agreement.

'Quite correct—and it's this early stuff, naturally, that's the most valuable.' He paused, glancing at Michael. 'You'll be able to tell him? You know the characteristics?'

'It's difficult, admittedly, but I think I can make a fairly accurate guess. I've handled some of this early stuff before.'

'You must be clever.' Delia's tones were suddenly crisp, and faintly sarcastic. 'And you're so young to be such an expert.'

'Michael's been in the business since he was fifteen,' Kathryn put in curtly. 'And his parents and grand-parents are also in the antique business.' She wondered if her dislike of Delia had revealed itself in her voice, for a rather uncomfortable little silence ensued. Then Michael said goodbye and moved to the door. Thankfully Kathryn followed him from the room.

'I think,' said John on the following Monday evening, 'I'll have that day in Derbyshire which you suggested.'

'You'll enjoy it,' Kathryn returned eagerly. 'The mountains and moors are really beautiful at this time of the year. When are you going?'

'Probably tomorrow, because this weather's too good to be true. It could break any time, and Mr Slade tells me the roads can be most treacherous when the mists come down.'

'That's true. They're narrow and you have long stretches where there are sheer drops on one side or the other.'

'Hmm. . . .' He paused thoughtfully. 'Yes, I'll

make it tomorrow. We'll start out very early and have a long day.'

'We?'

'It's not much use my going alone. You know the way, and the area.' They had just finished the accounts and were having supper in the sitting-room, before a glowing log fire. 'You can show me all the interesting places.'

'But—' With Michael's words about the possibility of an engagement between John and Delia still lingering in her mind, Kathryn could only stare at John for a moment, groping for words. A whole day out there on the moors, or wandering in the foothills of the mountains. . . . Surely he would prefer Delia's company, Kathryn thought, still unable to find anything to say.

'But—what?' He threw her a questioning glance. 'You're not doing anything particular, are you?'

She shook her head.

'Only the silver,' she murmured, already visualizing the trip, and at the same time becoming vaguely aware of a strange little fluttering of her pulse.

He smiled faintly at her.

'That can be done any time.'

'Yes, of course.' Kathryn picked up her cup and sipped her coffee. 'Are we taking our food?'

He raised his brows. Obviously roughing it on a hillside with a sandwich in his hand was not his idea of a pleasant meal.

'Are there no restaurants?'

'Not on the moors; the landscape's quite wild and vast areas are completely uninhabited, but we can go into Buxton or Matlock for lunch if you prefer it.'

'Yes, I do prefer it.'

They began discussing the trip, with John merely putting in the odd suggestion and for the most part leaving it to Kathryn to decide where they should go.

'The limestone area's the prettiest,' she told him.

'If you like caves there are several open; they're in the Castleton district.'

'That sounds attractive,' he nodded. 'And we can also do some tramping, can we?'

'Yes, it's the National Park; you can go anywhere you like.'

They were still talking when, half an hour later, the front doorbell rang. Kathryn heard Emily's voice, and then Delia Slade's softer, more husky tones. Kathryn's attention was with John; she saw his face relax and his eyes move expectantly to the door. Why, wondered Kathryn again, should he prefer her company on this trip into Derbyshire rather than Delia's?

'How cosy you both look!' Delia's voice was pleasant and her smile friendly, but Kathryn was conscious of the animosity lurking beneath her words. This intimate little scene was obviously a surprise to her.

'Let me have your things, Delia.' John got up to take them from her. 'Sit there,' he invited. 'I'll get another chair.' He draped her coat over the back of the couch and drew up another chair for himself. 'I didn't expect you this evening. There isn't anything wrong at home?'

'No, of course not. As a matter of fact Mother and Father are dining with some friends and I felt the need of company after sitting there, eating alone.'

'Why didn't you give me a ring? You could have come over here.'

'I did think of it, John, but I wondered if you'd be busy. Monday's your accounts day, isn't it?'

'That wouldn't have mattered. You know you're always welcome.'

After a little while Kathryn began to feel uncomfortable, for she was not brought into the conversation either by John or Delia, and at last she rose, saying she would take a walk in the grounds and then go to bed.

'Good night,' she said, turning at the door.

John answered quietly, smiling at her; Delia's answer was also spoken in softly-modulated tones, but in her gaze there was a mixture of triumph and mockery. No doubt about it, she was delighted at having driven Kathryn away.

Would John mention their outing? Kathryn wondered, and then dismissed the matter. She was walking by the lakeside; away on the rise lights in the dovecote glittered, reflecting themselves in the tiny stream that ran down from the hills to the lake. It was a beautiful night and Kathryn walked for over an hour. When she returned Delia was just leaving. She stood by the open door of her car, looking up at John who was standing close beside her.

'You'll be dining with us on Wednesday, then?' she was saying. 'We've some more friends coming whom we think you'd like to meet—' She broke off as Kathryn reached the steps leading to the front door. Her mouth compressed for a second before she added, smoothly, 'I hope you have a nice day tomorrow—both of you.' And with that she got into the car and drove away.

The sun was shining when Kathryn awoke the following morning; on looking out she saw that the mountain summits were covered with mist, but that was not unusual and she thought no more about it as, having taken a bath, she dressed in slacks and a sweater. She had washed her hair last night and it shone, framing her lovely face in gold. She used no make-up other than a hint of colour on her lips, for her cheeks were already enchantingly flushed, flushed with pleasure at the thought of a day up there on the moors, with the fresh wind caressing her face and the scent of heather in her nostrils.

John was also in casual attire, yet he appeared immaculate. Kathryn had never seen him otherwise, never seen so much as a hair out of place. But for all that he was thoroughly masculine . . . disconcertingly masculine, Kathryn decided when she saw him after breakfast. The deep tan of his skin, the intense blue of his eyes below dark straight brows, and the leanness of his stern, aristocratic face, all these added to the impression of masculinity, and Kathryn found herself thinking of the girl whom rumour had it he was intending to marry. Delia was so self-possessed, so superior and haughty, that Kathryn could not imagine her submitting to the demands and authority of her husband, yet anyone having John for a husband would most certainly be compelled to do that.

'Can I phone my mother?' Kathryn asked when they were almost ready to go. 'I'd just like her to know where I'm going—in case she should ring for some reason and wonder where I am.'

'I've told you before, Miss Ramsey, there's no need to ask my permission to use the telephone,' he replied with a flash of anger. 'Certainly use it—whenever you wish.'

She went away, biting her lip. Ever since the incident of the car she had made a point of asking permission before doing anything to which he could take exception. Her asking to use the telephone annoyed him, and he had in fact snapped at her like this once before, but Kathryn possessed an obstinate little streak which drove her to persist in this rather childish form of retaliation. Now she heartily wished she had used a little more tact, since it would not be a very pleasant drive if John were going to be in a bad temper.

But to her relief he seemed to have forgotten the incident as, taking the road out of Marbeck village, he turned right in the direction of Macclesfield. Passing through this town once famous for its silk, they soon found themselves on the narrow winding road off which ran the valley of the Goyt.

'If you turn left here,' Kathryn said, 'we come to a very pretty place. Part of the valley downstream was flooded recently to make a reservoir, but it's still very beautiful.'

Following her directions, John drove along a road with sheer drops, a road so narrow and winding that passing another car was a very hazardous business at times. However, there was little on the road at this time and they seemed to have the world of mountain and moorland to themselves. John pulled up at the head of the reservoir and they got out of the car.

'This was a lovely valley, and a settlement—'

'Settlement? People lived up here?' He shook his head. 'Not in this wild outlandish place!'

'They did,' she said with a grimace. 'It must have been a hard life, because the soil's so thin it must have been almost impossible to grow anything on it.' She paused, eyeing him uncertainly. 'I expect these mountains are just like small hills to you,' she went on, and to her surprise he laughed.

'They are,' he replied, but added, 'They're very beautiful, though, just as you said. I like your wild mountains and moorlands, Miss Ramsey.'

From there they went back the way they had come and drove on to Edale, once again leaving the car to walk to the famous swallet known as Giant's Hole down which flowed the water from Rushup Edge. The breeze came and dispersed the mist which had clung to the mountain summits, and Kathryn gave a little sigh of relief. She had been rather anxious, for it was never wise to ignore mist on these wild, uninhabited moorlands. It was so easy to lose one's bearings.

'Where do we go from here?'

'The Winnats Pass. We take this footpath.' John's large strides were taking him along far too fast and Kathryn began trotting to keep up with him.

'I'm sorry,' he smiled, slowing down to suit her pace. 'You're going to be breathless.'

'I don't easily tire—especially out here.'

'You come often?'

'Whenever I have the opportunity. There wasn't much time towards the end—when Mr Southon became ill, that was.'

'You'd extra work to do then, of course.'

She nodded, brushing a hand through her hair, for the breeze had tossed it into disorder. John's hair, she noticed, was somewhat awry too, but it merely added to his attractiveness and she stared at him, flushing as he looked down, a question in his eyes.

'Yes, Mr Southon's illness did entail extra work,' she said quickly. 'But I didn't mind.'

A little while later they were looking down the deep limestone gorge of the Pass, then they travelled on to the Blue John Mine.

'That's Mam Tor.' Kathryn pointed out the hill and then asked if he wanted to go into the mine. 'I think you'll like the Treak Cliff Cavern better,' she suggested, 'but we can go in both if you like.'

'We'll settle for the Treak Cliff Cavern.'

The area being one of high rainfall, numerous streams contributed to the spectacular underground drainage by which these beautiful caves were developed. There was a concentration of caves along the margins of the limestone, and more especially along the western and northern edges, for here the rock was reef limestone, which, owing to its purity, was highly soluble.

John seemed most interested, and by the time they came out of the Cavern all trace of that impersonal quality which was rarely absent from his make-up had disappeared. And after that there developed a friendly, almost intimate relationship between them. Perhaps it was the isolation, for as they tramped on again they were the only human beings in this vast and rugged domain. On reaching the car John sat for a moment regarding Kathryn with an almost quizzical expression.

'Did we say we'd have lunch in Buxton?' He glanced at his watch. 'Do you know what time it is?'

'I know it's long past lunch time,' she laughed. 'We'll have to call it afternoon tea.'

'We can call it that, but I'm hoping we can get something more substantial than scones and cakes.'

They managed to get a grill and, feeling much better for the meal, they came out into the main street of Buxton, got into the car, and continued on their way, driving up to the high moors. Eventually John stopped the car on a narrow verge and turned.

'How about another tramp?' He looked at her rather uncertainly. 'Are you tired?' he asked.

Kathryn shook her head.

'No, I'm not a bit tired.'

'Good, then we'll do some more walking.'

They strode briskly away, taking a sheep track into the hills.

'The heather—' Kathryn pointed to the purple heights in the distance. 'Isn't it beautiful?'

'Very. And those tumbling streams—this is a most charming landscape, Miss Ramsey.'

She smiled, trotting beside him, and feeling disproportionately happy. Nothing seemed important except the fact that she was here with John, and although she sensed a mist falling, it did not impress her deeply enough to awaken her to the possibility of danger.

Then suddenly it was there, masking the hills and swiftly enveloping the moors.

'We must turn back,' John said urgently, 'or we'll be completely lost.' But they had come a long way from the car, and Kathryn could not imagine their being able to reach it before visibility was cut down to only a few feet. They began to run, and as John was too fast for Kathryn he took her hand in order to help her along.

'We'll never make it,' she cried, breathless by this time. 'It's impossible. We've come too far.'

'The car's below, somewhere there—' John stopped for a second to peer downwards through the mist. And then to Kathryn's dismay he shook his head.

' You're right, Miss Ramsey, we'll never make it.' Nevertheless he began to run again, taking giant strides and pulling Kathryn along behind him. Her chest began to hurt, and then the hurt became a searing pain.

' I can't—can't—oh, I'll have to take a rest,' she almost sobbed. ' I'm so—so s-sorry.'

' It's not your fault, Kathryn. I shouldn't have run you off your feet like that. Take a rest and we'll go on again.'

Kathryn. . . . It registered, though only vaguely, for her whole mind was occupied with their plight.

' Do you know which way to go? ' she said, still gasping for breath.

' I think so. If only I can keep my bearings we're sure to find the car.'

' But if we find it you can't possibly drive in this,' she cried, wondering if they would ever get home at all that night.

' Perhaps not,' he admitted. ' But at least it will be more comfortable in the car than sitting on a hillside all night—'

' Sitting—? We can't do that!'

' I hope we won't have to.' A pause and then, anxiously, ' Can you go on now?'

' Yes, I'm all right.' She wasn't all right, but she managed to keep up with him as he began to walk in the direction which he surmised would lead them to the car. But by now the mist had become a thick grey fog; John reached for Kathryn's hand again, this time having to grope for it. She shivered and he said soothingly,

' Don't be frightened; we'll find the car eventually, though it might take some time.'

' But it's going dark as well,' she said, unconsciously tightening her hold on his hand. ' Oh, what will we do!'

' Don't be afraid,' he said again. ' If we can find the road we can start walking; we're bound to reach civilization some time.'

'I'm sure we won't find the road,' Kathryn murmured. They were walking together and yet John was only a vague dark shape beside her. Visibility could not be more than a few inches. 'How can we?'

John was silent, and they walked on—on and on, until at last he stopped.

'I've completely lost my direction,' he said, adding, 'I expect I lost it some time ago, but I kept on hoping we'd feel the gravel of the road beneath our feet. What's to be done now?' He paused in thought. 'There's a hut somewhere about here,' he said. 'I saw it as we came along—I expect you did too.' He moved this way and that, peering through the fog. Kathryn said fearfully,

'Aren't we going to try to find the car?'

'It's no use. The wisest thing is to search around for that hut; it isn't far away. We'll have to stay there for the night.'

'Stay—stay—' Kathryn choked and the words would not come for a while. 'Mr Hyland, we can't stay in a hut all night!'

'Would you prefer to wander around—with probably the danger of falling down a ravine?'

'No—oh, no!' she exclaimed swiftly.

'Well then. . . .' Still keeping hold of her, he moved about, always peering, searching for the hut. 'Ah,' he said at last, 'I see it.' The dark shape loomed up before them; soon they were stumbling over great stones and boulders that appeared to have fallen about the entrance. Once inside it seemed warmer, but it was only relative, and Kathryn shivered, for her clothes were damp and already her slacks were clinging to her legs, clammy and icy cold.

What time was it? Darkness had come down while they had been wandering about, but Kathryn guessed it wasn't much more than six o'clock. Twelve or fourteen hours . . . unless by some miracle the fog lifted before the morning.

John was bending down, and appeared to be scraping away at something.

' I've cleared a space here of the rubble,' he informed her at length. ' Give me your hand and I'll guide you to it; we'll have the wall to support our backs— Be careful, there are rocks and boulders everywhere.'

Extending her hand, Kathryn felt it taken in a firm and strangely comforting grip. She was carefully guided to the space he had cleared; gently he pushed her down, then eased himself on to the floor beside her.

Kathryn leant her back against the wall and, managing to stretch her own legs, she said in some concern,

' Are you comfortable? You can't stretch out, can you?'

' I'll manage. We'll have to sit close,' he went on matter-of-factly, ' both owing to the lack of space and in order to keep as warm as possible under the circumstances.'

' Yes . . . of course.' She was still shivering and without more ado John put an arm around her; she was drawn to him, feeling the warmth of his body . . . the warmth and the strength. What an odd situation, she mused, wondering what her companion was thinking. There had been so much dissension between them at one time or another, and now here they were, sitting like lovers, with the prospect of spending the whole night alone together in this tiny hut high on the Pennine moors.

' It might clear during the night,' she submitted hopefully at length, feeling the need for conversation. Sometimes it does—if the breeze get up, that is.'

' There's no sign of a breeze. No, Kathryn, we're here until daylight. Then we should be able to find the car.'

' We couldn't before,' she put in fearfully. ' It wasn't

86

dark when we first began searching, remember.' Panic seized her as her mind suddenly darted back to that time last year when the region had been completely cut off from civilization owing to its being blanketed in fog for over a week.

'It was late in the afternoon, though, and we hadn't much time before the dark eventually did beat us. To-morrow we'll have the whole day. Don't worry, we won't die up here.'

'I know that,' she retorted in faint protest. He re-mained so calm and unruffled, and Kathryn was filled with the desire to impart the impression that she was also accepting their position with the same cool resigna-tion. 'I was only thinking it could be just as difficult tomorrow as it was today—but, as you've said, we do have much more time.'

She fell to thinking again, her mind flitting from Delia to the servants at the Hall, and then to her own parents and sisters. What would people think? Tentatively she revealed her anxiety, though she did not mention Delia.

'What can they think? This was forced upon us. As for your parents, they won't ever know—unless you choose to tell them.'

'I'll have no need to,' she returned dismally. 'The report of this fog will be on the news, and when my mother hears it she's going to be anxious. She'll keep on ringing the Hall until I'm back.'

'I never thought of that. Pity you rang her this morning.'

'I regret it now,' she owned with a sigh, 'but there's nothing I can do about it. My parents will definitely know of this.'

He was silent for a moment, and Kathryn sensed the faint lift of his brows as he considered her words.

'Your parents trust you, I presume,' he remarked, and Kathryn's reply came swiftly,

'Certainly they trust me.'

'Well then, what are you worrying about? The servants at the Hall don't matter.' Kathryn had nothing to say to this and after a moment or two he went on, 'We might be able to sleep later, but for now —just relax. There's absolutely nothing we can do, so no amount of fretting is going to help.'

Kathryn gave a tiny sigh of resignation, deciding that if she must spend the night up on these grim and lonely moors, she would wish for no company more reassuring than that of this cool and unperturbed American.

CHAPTER V

She awoke and lay still, conscious of a choking sensation in her throat and a numbness in her feet and ankles. Where—?

John was beside her. The warmth of him; the way he held her so protectingly. He must have laid her down, clearing another space for her to stretch out. Had he slept? Kathryn lay there, staring up at the hole in the roof; then her eyes travelled to the opening which had once possessed a door of sorts. She could only just discern the aperture, for the fog was as dense inside as out.

'John—' she almost shouted, unaware of her slip. 'It hasn't cleared—not one little bit!'

'Give it time, child—'

'But it's light!' She sat up, feeling the sudden chill at the loss of his body warmth. 'Supposing we can't find the car and—and we have to stay another night.'

John sat up, then stood up; he stretched himself, then began moving his arms as if to release some ache from his muscles.

'We'll find the car all right.' He reached down and, quite naturally, Kathryn put her hand in his and dragged herself to her feet. 'What's the matter?' he inquired anxiously as she seemed to totter as if ready to fall.

'My ankles—they do hurt.'

John made her sit down again; he took off her shoes and began vigorously to massage her ankles.

'Better?' His tones were the familiar lazy drawl, but the depth of their anxiety could not be missed. How anxious he was . . . and how gentle his hands, despite their strength. Kathryn's heart fluttered oddly and she wondered if she would ever feel quite the same after this adventure.

'Yes, thank you—much better.'

'Lack of circulation. I did try to keep you as warm as I could, but you *would* pull your knees up and your feet were away from me. Do you always sleep curled up in a ball like that?' he added with some amusement, and Kathryn felt the colour come swiftly to her face.

'I expect I do, yes,' she murmured, very sure now that she would never feel quite the same.

'I think we'd better stay by the hut for a while,' John said as Kathryn waited uncertainly for him to suggest they move, and make some effort to find the road, even though the fog was still as dense as ever. 'Should it not lift, and we're forced to spend another night up here, at least we'll have some sort of shelter. If we leave the hut in this thick fog we'll never find it again.'

'Oh, but surely it will clear,' she cried, thinking of her parents, who were probably even now filled with deep anxiety as to her safety. 'Can't we just walk about —trying to find the road? It'll be better than doing nothing.'

He shook his head.

'If we leave the hut we'll never find it again,' he repeated. 'We'll walk about, by all means, if only to keep warm, but we mustn't stray far from here until this fog clears a little—until, in fact, we can be quite sure we're not going to need the hut again.'

Kathryn swallowed hard, but said nothing, and after a while he asked if she were hungry.

'I am, rather,' she admitted, 'and I'd give anything for a drink. The fog gets in your throat. You must be feeling it, too?'

'It is rather uncomfortable,' he owned, 'but for the time being at any rate, it's bearable.'

They walked about for over an hour, keeping the dim blur of the hut in view; when there was still no sign of the fog lifting John said something more positive must be done. He sounded faintly troubled, and Kathryn wondered if this were the reason for the sharpness of his voice when he spoke.

'You'll stay by the hut,' he said, 'while I go and see if I can find the road. We'll keep calling to one another; in this way there'll be no danger of our losing sight of the hut.'

He went off; Kathryn had never felt so alone, so completely isolated from all living things. He'd never find the road, she thought, although he did seem confident that it was not so very far away. Kathryn herself could not distinctly remember how long they had been walking before they came to the hut. They were chatting all the time and she had to admit to herself that she had been far more interested in her companion than her surroundings.

She heard him call and she answered. From then on his voice reached her at intervals, becoming less distinct all the time. Then she would hear it from a different direction, coming nearer. This went on for what seemed eternity and then, to her indescribable relief, she was instructed to leave the hut and go to him.

She ran, calling now and then, and stumbling at times, so great her haste to get through this fog and into the company of another human being. As she drew nearer another sound reached her ears. John was running the engine in order to get the heater operating.

'Oh, John—Mr Hyland,' she gasped, reaching him at

last. 'The car—I never thought you'd find it!'

If he noticed her slip he chose to ignore it as, opening the car door, he put a hand under her elbow and gently urged her inside. Then he was sitting in the driver's seat and the doors were closed.

'Warmer now?' He was regulating the heat and she felt it directed on to her feet and legs.

'Yes, thanks. That's wonderful—oh, it's dreadful to be so cold!'

'I'm sorry I wasn't quicker—it must have seemed a long time to you, standing around. But in actual fact it's only just after eleven now.'

'You can't drive in this,' Kathryn peered through the fog to discover if the road were in any way visible. 'No, you can't see at all.'

'It might lift. We'll give it another hour and then we're going to abandon the idea of using the car, and start walking. However, for the time being we're comfortable, and warm. Also—' he leant across her and opened the glove compartment, 'we have something to eat.'

'Food!' she exclaimed, as if she hadn't eaten for days. 'Oh, what?'

'Chocolate—a whole big bar of it. Here, help yourself.' He put it on her lap and, taking off part of the wrapping, Kathryn offered the chocolate to him.

'Thanks.' He helped himself and for a while they sat in silence, eating, and appreciating the warmth after the icy dampness of the crude lodging in which they had spent the night. 'Am I imagining things,' he asked suddenly, 'or is this fog beginning to lift?'

'I believe it is,' she returned breathlessly. 'Yes, look at it swirling; there's a breeze coming up.'

Five minutes later they were travelling along at snail's pace, John straining to keep the line of the verge in view. Several times Kathryn had to get out of the car and guide him. Time was passing far too quickly and darkness had begun to descend when at last they reached the road leading into Macclesfield.

'Just look at the lights,' Kathryn exclaimed. 'There's no fog at all down there!'

'No, it's only on the moors, apparently.'

It was almost seven o'clock when at last they drove up to the front door of the Hall. It was opened instantly by Burrows, whose weatherbeaten face was clouded with anxiety.

'Mr Hyland—Miss Ramsey—' He broke off, staring rather incredulously from John to Kathryn. They both looked much the worse for their experience, their faces being grimy from the fog, and their clothes, damp even before they'd slept in them, were creased and far from clean. John's suede shoes were stained and covered with a film of dust resulting from his efforts to clear part of the floor of the hut. Kathryn's shoes were even worse, for she had managed to stumble into a bog when running to the car. 'We were all so worried about you,' Burrows went on with admirable recovery.

'Thank you, Burrows, but you needn't have been. As you see, we're quite safe.' Despite his appearance John still retained his air of cool assurance. 'You know about the fog, I suppose?'

'Yes, sir.' Burrows closed the door before saying, hesitantly, 'You were trapped on the moors, sir?'

'We were—and very uncomfortable it was,' he remarked. 'I'm going up for a bath now. Put me some clean clothes out, will you?'

'Yes, sir—er. . . .'

'Well?' Already on his way to the stairs, John turned abruptly, his brows raised in inquiry.

'Miss Slade—she heard about the fog on the radio and rang last night. She rang again very late—about midnight. Then she's rung several times today. She said if you came in I must remind you you're dining with her and her parents tonight.'

Kathryn watched John's expression, but it remained noncommittal as he said,

' Thank you for the message, Burrows.' With that he strode briskly away and Burrows turned to Kathryn.

' Your mother, Miss Ramsey—she's been phoning as well. She's very anxious indeed about you, and it was all I could do to prevent her from getting in touch with the police. But I knew neither you nor Mr Hyland would like that sort of publicity.'

' Publicity?' For no apparent reason Kathryn's heartbeats quickened. ' What do you mean, Burrows?'

' Well, if the police had been called out to search for you—' He reddened and hesitated for a moment. ' It would have been in all the newspapers, wouldn't it?—on account of Mr Hyland being who he is.'

' I see. . . .' Regarding Burrows' face intently, Kathryn had no difficulty in reading his thoughts. ' I'll ring my mother at once,' was all she said, and went up to her room.

The telephone was by the bed and, picking up the receiver, Kathryn dialled the number.

Her sister Dawn answered the phone.

' Kathryn! Thank heaven you're safe! What happened? Mum's on her way over to the Hall—'

' On her way here? What for?'

' The lord knows. I told her she couldn't do anything, but you know Mum—she's always worrying about something or someone. She's been on tenterhooks ever since she heard about the fog on the news, and she would keep phoning the Hall all the time. Then about half an hour ago she jumped up and said she couldn't sit here doing nothing, so she made Dad drive her over.' A small pause and then, ''They should be there now—or they will be in a minute or two.'

Kathryn heaved a deep sigh.

' I wish I hadn't let her know I was going. She's been really worried, then?'

'Dreadfully.' A little silence followed and Kathryn had the impression that Dawn was carefully choosing her words. 'It was your being out with your boss that seemed to be half her trouble. . . .' There was a certain suggestiveness in her sister's tone which had the effect of making Kathryn bristle, and for this reason she remained silent, forcing Dawn to continue. 'What exactly happened? Did you have to stay at an inn, or something?'

Kathryn sat down on the bed; she held the receiver away from her and there was a moment of indecision as she stared at it, debating on whether or not to lie. However, she knew she could not do so convincingly; moreover, she would never lie to her parents, so there was nothing to be gained by withholding the truth from her sister.

'No, Dawn, we were trapped up on the moors—miles away from anywhere.'

'Trapped. . . . You mean, you were up there all night—with that handsome American? Where did you sleep?—out in the open?'

Kathryn's mouth compressed, for there was no mistaking the implication in her sister's words.

'We found a disused hut.'

'That was fortunate. And you slept there—just the two of you?'

'We slept there—just the two of us,' replied Kathryn with a sort of acid resignation.

'Coo. . . ! You lucky thing, Kate—'

'I didn't consider myself lucky,' she snapped, almost ready to cut her sister off. 'It was an awful position to be in.'

'Only because you're so staid,' Dawn scoffed. 'Most girls would have liked it enormously—and have taken advantage of it,' she added, a soft and subtle significance entering into her tone. 'Didn't you even let him kiss you?—or perhaps he didn't give you a choice? Did he try anything else? But he must have, they all do—'

Kathryn's hand was trembling; softly she replaced the receiver, but made no immediate move to take her bath. A glance across to the mirror revealed the paleness of her face. Dawn would even now be imparting the news to Rita; they would be discussing it and considering it a huge joke that their 'old-fashioned' sister had found herself in such a predicament. And it would be a good topic of conversation when they met their friends later this evening. In fact, Kathryn reflected dismally, the incident would very soon be public gossip 'on account of Mr Hyland being who he is' as Burrows had so transparently put it.

And what of her parents, especially her mother? She hated gossip, and would quite literally hang her head in shame at the idea of Kathryn's name being bandied about in this way.

Still, there was nothing to be done about it and at last Kathryn rose and went out of the room. Her parents would be here any moment now, Dawn had said, but Kathryn was determined they should not see her in this state and she hurried along the corridor to the bathroom. She had just reached it when Burrows came up the stairs.

'Miss Slade on the phone, Miss Ramsey,' he said. 'I told her Mr Hyland wasn't available just now and she asked to speak to you.'

Delia was the last person to whom Kathryn wanted to speak, but Burrows was expecting her to answer the phone and with a sigh of resignation she said,

'Thank you, Burrows. I'll take the call in my room.'

'So you're back?' Delia's voice was almost invidious in its softness. 'Burrows is the soul of discretion and closed up like a clam when I asked him what had happened. Obviously the fog prevented your returning last night, but what did you do? Did you stay the night in a hotel somewhere?' Still the softness in her tones, but an insistence also—an insistence on knowing all there

95

was to know. The inquiry, coming so soon after her sister's subtle implications, was almost more than Kathryn could stand and she wished fervently that she had refused to speak to Delia. How must she answer? Of a certainty John would not want Delia to learn the truth . . . and yet Kathryn felt convinced the truth could not be suppressed, not in a small country village like Marbeck. In any case, even though Burrows would obviously practise tact, this wouldn't be the case with Emily and Edna. They would without doubt relish the spreading of this little tit-bit of gossip among the villagers.

' I'm afraid I can't talk to you at the moment, Delia,' Kathryn apologized. ' I'm feeling rather spent, as you can imagine, and in fact I was just about to take a bath. Mr Hyland will be calling you in a little while, I'm sure.'

' He was dining with us this evening. Do you know if he's still coming?'

' No, I don't—but as I say, he'll be ringing you just as soon as he's bathed and changed.' Kathryn had no idea of her slips until Delia said, in tones as smooth as silk,

' You sound as if you're both the worse for wear.' There was a rather brittle pause, and then, in the same smooth voice, ' Where did you stay, Kathryn? Was it in Buxton?'

Anger surged over Kathryn; she said, without any effort at politeness,

' You'll have to question Mr Hyland, Delia. I'm sorry, but I'm going to ring off now.' With that she once again placed the receiver on its rest.

After a hasty bath and complete change of clothes Kathryn was in her room, brushing her hair, when Emily called from the other side of the door.

' Your mother and father are here, Miss Ramsey. Shall I take them into the sitting-room?'

' Yes, please, Emily. I'll be down in a moment or two.' The maid's footsteps died away; athryn kept on brushing her hair, trying to still the thumping of her heart. This was ridiculous, she told herself angrily; what had happened out there on the moors could have happened to anyone—in fact it often had—so why should she be submerged in this feeling of guilt? With an angry gesture she replaced the brush on the tray and, touching her lips with a hint of colour, she went down to face her parents.

' Kathryn. . . .' Mrs Ramsey appeared to be ready to cry with relief. ' Oh, how glad we were to get here and find you'd arrived back safely! I was so sure you'd got completely lost and fallen down a gorge, or into a river or something.' She had risen from her chair, but instantly sank back in it. ' Child, what happened? I wanted to get the police to send out a search party, but Mr Burrows became actually angry at the suggestion.' A determined light entered her eyes. ' We came here to see him, and to tell him we weren't going to wait any longer, because it said on the radio that the fog up there was as bad as ever.' Kathryn was standing by the door, watching her father. He had been anxious, that was plain, but now he was quite calm, much more calm than his wife, who still seemed to be on the verge of tears. ' What happened, dear? Sit down and tell us all about it.'

Kathryn obeyed, sitting between them. Words were difficult at first, but she managed to give them a complete picture of what had happened.

' It seemed like a nightmare at first,' she ended, even managing a light-hearted laugh. ' But now it's all over it doesn't seem so very bad at all.'

' Not bad?' Her mother gaped at her. ' But—but you've just told us you spent the night in a hut with your employer—'

' Just a minute,' her husband interposed swiftly as the colour flooded Kathryn's cheeks. ' You mustn't say things like that, Mother—not about our daughter. What happened couldn't be helped. She's done no wrong.'

'I'm not saying she has,' quivered his wife. 'But the neighbours—the gossip—oh, why couldn't you have stayed at an inn, or even a cottage?'

'There didn't happen to be an inn or a cottage anywhere about,' Kathryn replied patiently.

'If the gossip's worrying you like this,' Mr Ramsey put in, 'then what's to prevent us from saying they did stay at a hotel?'

'But they've no proof.'

'Proof?' Her husband frowned in puzzlement. 'Why should proof be necessary?' he asked, and it was some moments before Mrs Ramsey was able to answer his question.

'The newspaper,' she faltered. 'I—when Mr Burrows was so against my going to the police I phoned the *Chronicle*, thinking they could do something—'

'The *Chronicle*!' Kathryn stared at her mother in dismay. 'You didn't let them know that we were lost?' The local rag! This was worse than anything.

Contritely her mother shook her head.

'I was so frightened. I felt I must do something.'

'You never mentioned this to me.' Mr Ramsey's voice took on an unaccustomed sternness and his mouth became tight. 'Why did you do a thing like that without telling any of us?'

'I was nearly out of my mind with worry. It's no use looking at me like that, James! I just couldn't sit there doing nothing.'

'The—the reporter will be round to see Mr Hyland.' Kathryn trembled at the prospect of John's reaction to a thing like that. He would be furiously angry, for publicity of this kind would naturally be most distasteful to him, more especially as rumours of his forthcoming engagement to Delia were now freely circulating. What of Delia herself? Would she throw him over? Impatiently Kathryn dismissed all thought of Delia, for there were other, more important matters on her mind. She looked pleadingly at her father, who was still regarding his wife with that stern expression on his otherwise good-humoured face. 'Can't we do something? They mustn't come here, Father. Mr Hyland will be so angry. Will you go along to the office and see the manager, or some-one? Tell them we're quite safe, and that it was all a mistake?'

'I'll go, certainly,' he said, though at the same time heaving a little sigh of doubt. 'But you know what they are; anything about the lord of the manor is always news, and in this case they'll be more eager than ever to publicize the incident, owing to Mr Hyland's having inherited the place in the way he did. You remember the publicity going on at the time it was discovered that this American was the heir to Marbeck, don't you?' He shrugged. 'I'll do what I can, naturally, but I haven't much hope, Kathryn. I'm sorry, lass.'

Kathryn's lips quivered. She reflected on the sense of companionship that had come to her and John as they tramped the moors. They had eaten a meal together and visited the Cavern, and then they had tramped again, and during all that time Kathryn knew that John's enjoyment was as great as her own. Then in the danger which followed there had been a strange close-ness, born of the knowledge that their plight could be-come disastrously worse, should the fog persist for any length of time.

Then there was the night itself, when they had been forced to sleep as close as lovers, in order to keep warm. From all this had come a friendliness in which John's previous austerity of manner towards her had no place. It had disappeared for ever—or so Kathryn had believed. But now. . . . Not only would there be a return of that cool austerity, but there would in all probability be a most unpleasant scene when John discovered what her mother had done.

'If only I hadn't told the newspaper,' Mrs Ramsey

cried, cutting into Kathryn's thoughts. 'The scandal —I shan't be able to ever hold my head up again. My daughter, to be talked about—I never thought to see a thing like that!'

'It's your own doing,' snapped Mr Ramsey, his patience running out. 'You knew very well what the result would be. To contact the press—it was a most stupid thing to do!'

'I thought they might help—send out a search party. The newspapers often do, you know—'

'Not a paper like the *Chronicle*! They've no money for that sort of thing.'

'No? Well, I never stopped to consider that. I was so afraid Kathryn might be lying at the bottom of some great cliff, all alone, and probably dying!'

'I wasn't alone,' Kathryn reminded her, more curtly than she intended. 'Mr Hyland was with me.'

'Yes, but you could have fallen down the cliff, just the same. And what could he have done?'

'He'd have done something, I can assure you of that.' The promptitude of her reply brought her father's head round in swift and puzzled inquiry. Kathryn remained silent and he turned to his wife.

'I think,' he said quietly, 'that we'd better be going. There's nothing to stay for, now that we know our daughter's safe.' He smiled affectionately at Kathryn, then rose to his feet. 'Come on, Mother. The best thing you can do now is to forget all about it.'

'Forget?' She got up from the chair. 'It'll be a long time before this is forgotten. The worst is to come yet —when the gossips really get going. The things people will say, and about you, who've never given me a moment's anxiety! I don't know how I'm going to bear it!' To Kathryn's utter dismay her mother burst into tears.

'Don't cry—you mustn't.' Rising, Kathryn slipped an arm round her mother's waist. 'True, there'll be scandal and gossip, but it'll be forgotten in no time at all. Now just you stop this worrying. I'll be along on Tuesday evening as usual, and I want to see you smiling, understand?'

'You sound as if you don't care,' Mrs Ramsey began when Kathryn interrupted her.

'Certainly I care. It's going to be awful. But what about Mr Hyland? He's going to suffer more than I, much more, because of his position.'

'People don't condemn men the way they do women. It's your name that'll be besmirched, not his. It'll be —be dragged in the mud!'

'I understand that,' Kathryn admitted, a note of fear entering her voice in spite of a resolve to accept the situation with equanimity. 'But I'll just have to ignore the gossip and—and hold my head up.'

'I'll never hold mine up,' her mother declared tragically. 'This is going to be with us for the rest of our lives!'

'Don't be silly—'

'And as for you—' Mrs Ramsey actually glared at her husband, 'I don't believe you're in the least concerned about your daughter's reputation.'

'Naturally I'm concerned, but this thing's happened and there's nothing we can do about it.'

'I still think Mr Hyland's going to suffer more than I—'

'Neither of us is going to suffer.' The lazy drawling tones startled them all and three heads turned swiftly in John's direction. He stood by the door, hands thrust carelessly in the pockets of a loose-fitting jacket of beige linen. He appeared to have been listening for some time; he also appeared faintly bored by the whole affair, for he drew one brown hand from his pocket to suppress a yawn. Then, extending the hand in Kathryn's direction, he gave a peremptory little gesture of his head. Mechanically, Kathryn obeyed the silent command and, moving towards him in a very dazed fashion, she slipped her hand into his. She looked up at him, towering almost up to the great oak beams. His blue eyes glinted as they became fixed on her scared and pallid countenance. 'First, my dear, you'd better introduce me to your parents,' he suggested, an odd sort of smile hovering about his lips.

'Y-yes, of course.' Kathryn felt as if she were in some sort of dream, standing there holding John's hand, just as she had held it up there on the moors, when they dared not let go, for fear of losing one another.

'I'm most pleased to meet you both,' John said graciously when Kathryn had stammered out the introductions. 'And now, to prevent all that scandal, to set all our minds at rest—Kathryn and I are to be married.'

The air was electrified. Kathryn gave a little gasp and her thoughts flew to Delia. Her parents just gaped at John, dumbstruck. As was to be expected, Mrs Ramsey was the first to recover, and the brightness in her eyes was not all the result of her recent tears as she said, in a voice edged with faint hysteria, despite its eagerness,

'Married? You'll marry Kate?—in order to save her reputation?'

John threw her a flickering smile.

'I think you exaggerate, Mrs Ramsey. The consequences of our unfortunate experience could never be as calamitous as you've suggested. Your daughter's name would never be dragged in the mud, I'm sure. However, scandal and gossip are always to be avoided if possible, for the memory does remain, as you have previously stated, for a very long while. As neither Kathryn nor I wish to carry this kind of stigma, there's only one thing to be done. We must announce our engagement immediately.' He turned to her then and added, rather in the manner of an afterthought, 'I trust this suggestion meets with your approval?'

She swallowed, trying to clear her throat. Words came

at last, though with the utmost difficulty.

'It's such a surprise, Mr—' She broke off, looking at him timidly, as if seeking permission to use his name. He responded by the merest increase of the pressure on her hand and she went on, 'I don't know what to say. I didn't expect—I mean, there's no need for you to—to make this sacrifice.'

'I've already stated, my dear, that the engagement will set *all* our minds at rest. I've no more desire than you to be subjected to the sort of derision which would result from gossip of this kind. No, Kathryn, it will be no sacrifice on my part.' He turned to her father, who had been studying Kathryn's face with an odd expression in his eyes. 'How about you, Mr Ramsey? I think you'll agree this is the most effective way of checking the gossip even before it starts?'

Mr Ramsey looked up at him and said gruffly,

'It will be effective, no doubt of that.' His glance flickered to Kathryn. 'If this is what my girl wants?'

Kathryn stared at him, his last words impressing themselves on her mind more than any others that had been spoken this evening. 'If this is what my girl wants?'. Did she want to marry John? She thought of that first meeting and the resulting antagonism which John had shown towards her. She recalled the increased friction when she had insisted on his observance of the provision made for her by Mr Southon. But these lost their importance beside times like those they had spent together in the Library, like the evening when she and Michael had sat with John discussing paintings . . . and like yesterday. Kathryn's thoughts then strayed to Delia. What were John's feelings for her? Surely they could not be strong, otherwise he would be quite unable to give her up. Yet he did seem to have developed some sort of affection for her. And what of Delia's feelings for John? That she desired to marry him Kathryn had no doubt, but whether or not she loved him was another matter altogether. Kathryn felt convinced Delia was totally incapable of loving deeply—but at the same time she was honest enough to own that her dislike of the girl always influenced her estimation of Delia's character.

'It isn't a matter of what she wants, but what is best for her.' Kathryn's musings were abruptly brought to an end by the anxious voice of her mother, who sounded as if she still had in mind Kathryn's small protest that John had no need to marry her. 'Mr Hyland knows what's best, James, so I feel we mustn't interfere.'

Glancing up to note the effect of this on John, Kathryn was most embarrassed to see his lips curve in a smile half amused, half sardonic.

The eager mother, anxious to marry her daughter off to a wealthy man. Was that what he was thinking? Kathryn had no doubt of it and her chin lifted. Here they all were, settling her future, arranging a marriage —and she, it appeared, was to submit meekly to whatever plans they chose to make for her. Her chin went higher. She would face the scandal; she would flatly refuse to marry John— 'If this is what my girl wants?' Her father's words interrupted her rebellious thoughts and she cast John a glance from under her lashes. His piercing blue eyes were fixed upon her. Had he seen that defiant lift of her chin? She felt sure he had even before he said, rather in the tones one might use to a fractious child,

'Come, Kathryn, you haven't answered me. Has my suggestion your approval?' He smiled at her, the kind of smile she had never seen on his lips before, and as if impelled by some force stronger than herself—she said, in clear decisive tones,

'Yes—John, your suggestion has my approval.'

CHAPTER VI

'You don't have to do it.' In spite of her agreement
to John's suggestion Kathryn turned to him immediately
upon her parents' departure. 'Father might be able to
prevent the account appearing in the newspaper.'

'It's already too late.' John regarded her in a sort
of silent reproach and Kathryn waited in some bewilderment for what was to come next. 'Why did you give
your sister all the details so soon? It would have been
far more prudent to have kept silent—at least until we'd
talked about the matter.'

'I—' Kathryn stared. 'How do you know I've been
speaking to Dawn?'

'The reporter's already been on the phone. Apparently he belongs to the same crowd as your sister. She
talked—as was to be expected,' he added on a faintly
disparaging note, 'and the fellow promptly contacted
me. Why did you tell her?' he asked again.

'I wouldn't have,' she returned hastily, the colour
rising at the idea of his supposition that she could not
hold her tongue. 'Burrows said Mother was anxious
and naturally I telephoned to let her know I was safe.
Dawn answered and—and asked questions. . . .' Kathryn
tailed off miserably. 'I'm so sorry.'

'Couldn't you have prevaricated?'

'I suppose I didn't give it enough thought.' She
shook her head, staring up at him through eyes shadowed
with contrition. 'I couldn't have lied, could I?'

His mouth compressed, but after a while he said, in
tones much softer than she expected,

'No, Kathryn, you couldn't have lied.' He shrugged
resignedly. 'It would have come out anyway, even if
your mother hadn't gone to the press, so don't go worrying yourself about it. Come on, let's eat. I'm ravenous,

and I'm sure you are too.'

How cool and unconcerned he appeared; it was almost as if he had no regrets whatever about the marriage. But that could not possibly be so, for it would be a marriage of convenience only; there would be nothing in it for him . . . or for her.

'We've no need to do it,' she cried impulsively. 'The gossip will soon die down, it always does!'

'I think we've already decided the gossip will not very quickly die down,' he commented, watching her with an odd expression in his eyes. 'A short while ago you agreed to my suggestion. Have you changed your mind? Are you afraid of marrying me?'

Something in his tone brought her head up with a jerk.

'Afraid? No—but you can't really want to marry me.'

'You can't want to marry me, for that matter,' he countered smoothly. 'But as neither you nor I have any desire to be the object of unsavoury gossip it's a necessity.' Again that air of unconcern. He appeared to have forgotten Delia's existence altogether! Delia. . . . Kathryn looked apologetically at him and told him Delia had phoned.

'I said you'd ring her back. You should have dined with the Slades.'

'So I should, but they'll understand. I'll ring later. Come on, child, let's eat.'

It was the first time John had asked her to dine with him, although he was well aware that she had dined regularly with her previous employer. She had been more one of the family then, but now she was merely a servant—Kathryn's heart jerked. In the turmoil of her mind there had been no realization of her changed position. Now, as the knowledge filtered through, her eyes glowed, in spite of herself. To be here always, mistress of the lovely stately home to which she had become so attached . . . to be the lady of the manor. . . .

Such an exalted position. Could she fill that position in the way her husband would expect of her? Trembling now, she let her knife drop to her plate with a clatter which seemed to fill the whole vast Dining Room. Even the branch of silver candlesticks echoed musically to the sound. John looked up interrogatingly and Kathryn swiftly apologized.

'What are you thinking of?' he queried, frowning. 'You look scared out of your wits.'

'I was wondering—' Her hands still trembled; she glanced across at him with great doubt and apprehension in her eyes. 'John . . . will I be able to fit in, do you think?' She was pleading, although quite unaware of it—pleading like a frightened child for words of reassurance. She looked rather like a child too, with her cloud of fair hair falling about her face, and little lines of anxiety creasing her wide, intelligent brow.

'You've fitted in very well up till now.' He smiled at her, in a very special way, and she gasped. Never would she have credited him with such understanding. 'It isn't as if you're not used to the life here.' He shook his head. 'You need have no misgivings, Kathryn, I have great faith in you.'

'Oh . . . thank you.' At her swift response and grateful glance his smile broadened. A change had undoubtedly occurred in him as a result of that day and night up on the moors, and Kathryn dwelt for a space on their forthcoming marriage. A marriage of convenience, she had concluded, unable to see beyond that; a marriage in which there would be nothing for either of them. But now she wondered. . . . Perhaps, later. . . .

'I'll ring Delia,' John said, when they had finished dinner. 'Go into the Drawing Room; I'll be with you in a few minutes.'

Kathryn sat on the chair by the fire, waiting for John to join her, and wondering how he would break the news to Delia. The Slades would be bitterly disappointed, for they had clearly been hoping for a marriage between Delia and John. As for Delia herself, Kathryn refused to dwell on what her reaction to John's engagement would be, for in addition to the familiar patronage she extended towards Kathryn, there had lately been an added hostility which Delia hadn't taken the slightest trouble to hide.

Kathryn looked up as John entered the room. His face was taut and at the corner of his mouth there were little lines of white showing through the deep tan of his skin. Was he very upset? Kathryn wondered, suddenly dejected. On the surface there had been a calm acceptance of the necessity of marriage to the girl who was merely an employee, but underneath it all there must surely be the wish that he could have had a choice, could have married a woman more suitable—and who would also be a wife in more than name only.

Her anxiety was instantly communicated to him and, as he passed her chair to take the one at the other side of the fireplace, his hand came on to her shoulder and she knew the welcome reassurance of his grip.

' I'm having this room for ourselves from now on,' he said, deliberately ignoring the timid inquiry of her gaze. ' It's all very well to have these lovely rooms on show, but this particular one pleases me and I'm keeping it private.'

' It is a beautiful room,' Kathryn agreed. ' I'm glad you're having it for yourself—' She broke off, an involuntary laugh rising to her lips. And all at once her shyness and unnatural restraint dissolved as she said, correcting her mistake, ' I'm glad we're having it for our own use, John.'

As Kathryn had told him on that first day, the Drawing Room had, right down through the centuries, been the principal living room at Marbeck Hall, and as she sat there, gazing dreamily into the fire, Kathryn tried to visualize those bygone days of glory, when the ' fighting

Fittons' had sat here discussing some campaign in which they had been engaged—or were going to be engaged.

'Where are you now?' John demanded, startling her out of her dream.

Kathryn laughed.

'I was just wondering what we'd hear if sounds could come back—' She broke off, wrinkling her brow. 'Was it Marconi who said no sound is ever lost?—that it all survives in the ether?'

'I believe it was—yes, I'm sure of it.' He glanced towards the door as Emily entered with the coffee tray. She placed it on the table by the fire, then after a curious and rather searching glance at Kathryn, she left the room. 'Tell me,' John invited as Kathryn began pouring the coffee, 'what do you imagine we'd hear, were we able to recapture those sounds that are supposed to be still floating about in the ether?'

'Well . . . I imagine we'd hear Sir Edward Fitton proudly discussing his grandfather's campaign in the Wars of the Roses—how Sir Thomas was knighted for valour at the Battle of Blore Heath. He took about seventy Marbeck men with him on that day and over thirty were killed.'

'Yes, and what else?' He held out his hand for the coffee she was passing to him. 'What about the great Sir Edward Fitton, the one you said was a friend of Queen Elizabeth?'

'He was the one of the "haughy countenance and contempt of superiority",' she laughed, and went on to tell John more about the life of this Edward Fitton who became one of England's great officers of state. 'Many of the Fitton men held important offices and, therefore, included royalty among their friends.'

'And what about the Fitton women? Tell me what gossip and small talk of theirs is sprinkling the atmosphere up there above the clouds.' He put his coffee cup to his lips and regarded her from over the rim, his blue eyes flickering with amusement.

'I expect the talk of Mary would be interesting,' she said on impulse. 'As you know, she became Maid of Honour to the Queen, but her brilliant career was cut short by—by the misfortune that overtook her.' Odd, she mused, but never before had she felt embarrassed on relating the story of Mary's misdemeanour.

'Ah, yes; she and the Earl of Pembroke were to dwell in the Tower, so you said.' John was laughing and Kathryn responded, nodding in answer to his question.

They sat through the evening, Kathryn relating incidents in the history of the Hall, and the famous men and women who made that history. At ten o'clock John stifled a yawn and announced his intention of going to bed, advising Kathryn to do likewise.

'It will do us good to go early,' he observed, getting up from his chair. 'It'll make up a little for what we lost last night.'

The engagement coming only a few months after Mr Hyland had taken up residence at Marbeck Hall, made front page headlines in the *Chronicle*, while the report of the mishap up on the moors occupied a mere half a dozen lines near the end of the report. This was followed by the statement that although the ordeal must have been most trying for the couple, it had had a most happy sequel. All their friends, and especially the numerous visitors to the Hall who knew Miss Ramsey personally, would be relieved to learn they were little the worse for their ordeal, and delighted by the news of the engagement.

Congratulations poured in; Kathryn was overwhelmed by the good wishes she received from the visitors, and her eyes were actually bright with tears when she read the letter from Mrs Percival. It was signed by all the other old people whom she had assisted at their time of difficulty. After the congratulations on her engagement, and her good wishes for the future, Mrs Percival had gone on to express sincere thanks for what Kathryn had done for her and the others in their plight.

Amused by her emotion, John insisted on reading the letter.

'It's only for me,' she began when he interrupted her.

'Is it a congratulatory letter?' Kathryn nodded and he held out his hand. With a shrug of resignation she gave it up, and then watched his face intently as he perused Mrs Percival's rather spidery writing. At last he raised his eyes. 'Why didn't you explain?' he demanded, with a little flash of anger.

'I did try to, John, but I'm afraid I wasn't very convincing. You see, they're all old, and most of them have no relatives. If I hadn't let them come here those who were without relatives would probably have had to go into an institution, because they hadn't any money to speak of.'

John handed her back the letter; as she took it he gripped her hand.

'Tell me about your sisters,' he asked. 'They were turned out of their flat, you said?'

'There isn't really any excuse about them,' she was bound to confess. 'I know from experience how rowdy they are—Mother wouldn't have them at home for that reason. But they are my sisters, so I offered them rooms here. I thought they'd stay only a couple of weeks or so, until they found another flat.'

'I see.' To her astonishment he pulled her to him and before she could collect herself he had bent his head to kiss her lightly on the brow. 'I misjudged you, didn't I?' He retained her hand, and to her extreme embarrassment the paper she held began to flutter. 'I'm sorry, my dear. You must forgive me for not being a little more patient about the whole affair.'

'It wasn't your fault at all,' she hastily argued. 'You had every right to be angry—anyone would have been, coming here and finding all that going on—' She stopped, dismayed, for that skit was the last thing of which she wanted to remind him. But she had gone too far; the sudden compression of his lips told her that. 'I'm so sorry, John,' she added unhappily. 'We were given a totally wrong impression by the newspapers; we thought—' She gestured self-deprecatingly. 'That's no excuse, for the new owner was entitled to respect, no matter who he turned out to be.'

A small silence followed her contrite declaration; John still held her hand and after a while he gave it a little squeeze.

'I think we must forget all that and begin again,' he said decisively. And he added, looking down steadily into her eyes, 'Our marriage is not based on love, Kathryn, and for that reason we shall most likely encounter difficulties; we must not risk the added complications either of animosity on my part or of a sense of guilt on yours. From this moment all that's happened in the past is to be forgotten, understand?'

She nodded, thinking how wise he was, and how practical. At the same time she was astute enough to guess that although he had referred only to guilt on her part, he was also telling her she must forget any animosity she might have felt for him; animosity resulting from his treatment of her when, in retaliation for her stubborn insistence on remaining at the Hall, he had made her do such menial tasks as waiting on the Slades. But little did he know that she had forgotten it already, that it had all faded into insignificance from the moment he had changed towards her when, in his new friendliness and consideration, she had seen the promise of his retaining her services. She had to smile at the recollection, for that was all she desired—to remain at the Hall as his employee. And now here she was, remaining at the Hall as his wife!

Kathryn's thoughts reverted to his statement that their

marriage would not be based on love and therefore they might encounter difficulties. What were these difficulties? she wondered, for the first time feeling she had perhaps been too precipitate in accepting John's offer of marriage. 'I shall try, though,' she whispered to herself. 'I shall try very hard—and perhaps, some day, he'll come to care for me a little.'

John was still watching her with that steadfast expression; she smiled, saw his eyes soften, and all her doubts were quelled. Difficulties there might be, but if John could look at her like this then there was a very good chance of surmounting those difficulties.

'I've to go into Macclesfield on business,' he said, interrupting her thoughts, and he added, 'I shan't be sorry when the house is closed for the winter. It'll be nice to have it to ourselves for a while—and to have a rest from these accounts.'

Was he contemplating closing it altogether? Kathryn wondered, watching him ease into the car before driving away down the road. It was a pleasant change having the house closed during the winter months, but always Kathryn had looked forward eagerly to the spring when, with the gardens ablaze with colour, the house had once more been thrown open and the crowds had come, thinly at first, but increasing as the days lengthened and became warmer.

As she stood by the window another car swung into the drive—Delia's car. Kathryn's pulses quickened in spite of herself. But almost at once her head tilted proudly and although she would obviously have preferred this visit to have taken place when John was in, she was determined to hold her own with this girl who, ever since John's coming, had adopted a most supercilious air towards her and, more recently, treated her with open hostility.

Emily had let her in; Kathryn heard the inquiry for Mr Hyland. She heard Emily's reply and the next moment Emily appeared at the door of the room.

'Miss Slade's here, Miss Ramsey.'

'Show her in, please, Emily.'

But Delia was in, standing just inside the door, her arrogant eyes sweeping over Kathryn from head to toe and then coming to rest on her face. Stepping aside to allow Emily to leave, she began to peel off her gloves.

'Aren't you going to invite me to sit down?' she asked with a deliberate raising of her brows which was meant to remind Kathryn of her lack of courtesy.

'You usually sit down without being invited,' came the smooth rejoinder. 'However, please do have a seat.' Kathryn sat down herself, and folded her hands in her lap. 'John isn't in—but Emily did inform you of that.'

Delia leant back in her chair with a languid movement which somehow reminded Kathryn of a panther, sleek, loose-muscled—ready to pounce and claw at its prey.

'I suppose I should congratulate you,' she said with sarcasm. 'And offer my condolences to John.'

'I don't think I understand?' Despite her apparent composure Kathryn seethed inwardly at the downright rudeness of Delia's subtle implication. 'Why, might I ask, should my fiancé require your sympathy?'

Delia actually flinched at the use of the word fiancé, and any doubts that Kathryn had as to whether or not Delia had cherished hopes of marrying John were instantly dispelled.

'Are you trying to tell me he's in love with you?' queried Delia with a sneer.

'I wasn't aware that I'd tried to tell you anything, Delia,' returned Kathryn quietly. 'I asked you a question, which you haven't answered.'

'You're almost insolent!' Delia's hand, resting on the arm of the chair, clenched so that her knucklebones shone through the creamy whiteness of her skin. 'Obviously John's to be pitied—a man in his position having to marry a girl like you. All this newspaper talk of romance,' she went on, her lips curling in a sneer. 'It suits the villagers and tenants; they take it in. But anyone with any intelligence can guess what's happened. In John's own circle he'll be the object of pity, and what's more, Kathryn, they're not going to accept you.'

This last statement caused the colour to leave Kathryn's cheeks, and her heart began to race uncomfortably. Had John considered this aspect of their marriage? True, he had not made a great number of friends as yet, but from the first invitations had poured in and Kathryn was sure that immediately the house was closed and John had more free time, he would accept these invitations and discriminately gather around him a circle of friends of his own class and culture.

'John's thought of all that.' The assumed air of confidence was ineffective, for Delia shook her head emphatically. 'He asked me to marry him, so he must have,' Kathryn added with a little toss of her head.

'You're actually trying to convince yourself that he really wants to marry you!' Delia's harsh laugh grated on Kathryn's ears; she tried to forget it as she said, in the same controlled tones,

'John did want to marry me, Delia. He's not the sort of person to make a wrong or hasty decision.'

'Nonsense! He can't want to marry you— Why, you've been out of favour with him right from the beginning, and if you'd had any pride you'd have gone when he wanted you to.' She leant forward, and her voice was an invidious purr as she added, 'He's being gallant and saving you from disgrace, but at what a sacrifice to himself. Are you intending to let him make that sacrifice?'

Kathryn's blue eyes sparkled, but she curbed her rising anger, for some instinct warned her to beware of this girl for whom John's feelings were friendly, to say the least. It was not feasible that John would drop the Slades, simply because he had become engaged to

Kathryn. There would undoubtedly be times when John and Delia talked together, and Kathryn made a silent resolve to say nothing which could be twisted by Delia, and then related to John.

' You've guessed why we're marrying, so I won't deny that it's owing to the gossip which would have followed upon the news of our staying together on the moors all night. But John's decision was made with the object of saving himself, as well as me. He has a high position to maintain, as you implied, and talk of that kind would be most humiliating for him. So you see, Delia, he's not being gallant, but has chosen the most sensible way out of the situation; he's done it not only for me, but for us both.'

Delia's eyelids fluttered down, and for some reason Kathryn went over what she had just said, wondering if there were any words at all which Delia could twist. She could not discover anything and she dismissed the idea that Delia was silently endeavouring to commit every word to memory.

' I still maintain he's doing it entirely for you,' Delia said. ' And if you allow him to ruin his life in this way, then you're asking for trouble. He's bound to regret it—and before very long.' The merest pause followed, and Kathryn waited breathlessly for Delia to continue. ' You must have guessed, Kathryn, that John and I were about to announce our engagement very soon?'

' I—I had heard—rumours,' Kathryn quivered, her composure beginning to desert her in spite of her determination to retain it. ' But if—if John cared so very much for you he—couldn't—couldn't marry someone else, whatever had happened.'

' John's a gentleman; he firmly believes he owes you marriage. I think you've learned enough about him to realize he would never put himself first in a situation of this kind. No, Kathryn, he'll forfeit his own happiness, but, as I've said, he'll regret it . . . and so will you if you continue with this ridiculous engagement.'

Kathryn stared at her, wondering if she were as white as she felt. Even her lips felt drained of colour and a dryness had gripped her throat, making speech impossible for the moment. She stood up, turning her back to Delia, her eyes wandering over the lovely undulating lawns and over to the high tilting ground above which came a glimpse of the fringe-like line of ancient trees bordering the far boundary of the Great Park. Was this all really for her? Would she find happiness?—or would John eventually come to regret his action, as Delia so emphatically maintained?

Had the engagement between Delia and John been a certainty? Rumours usually had some factual basis, although in this case they could easily have stemmed from the local gossip of the servants, for Delia was a fairly regular visitor to the Hall, and John often dined at the Slades'.

Delia sighed impatiently and Kathryn turned; unconsciously she twisted the lovely diamond and ruby ring on her finger . . . and her eyes opened wide at the malevolence of Delia's gaze as it became fixed on her hand before, lowering her head, Delia strove to hide her expression. Kathryn gasped; she knew, without any doubt at all, that this girl would harm her if she could; yes, and she would go to any lengths in order to do so.

'Are you going to adopt the sensible course and take my advice?' Delia's voice was brittle, her eyes narrowed half expectantly.

Kathryn raised her brows.

'You haven't proffered any advice, Delia.'

The older girl's eyes raked Kathryn's slender figure arrogantly.

'How cool you are—or pretend to be. Here's my advice, Kathryn, and it will be to your cost if you don't take it: give John up!'

Kathryn shook her head.

'I'll not take your advice, Delia. I'm staying engaged to John for as long as he wants me to.'

'And you'll marry him, knowing he loves me?'

'I'll marry him. . . .' Kathryn's voice quivered off into silence, despite her supreme effort at composure. For all the animosity that existed between them, Kathryn had never thought to endure a scene such as this.

'You won't marry him, I'll see to that!' Delia spoke impulsively, regretting her words on the instant. But she had said them, and Kathryn stared in blank bewilderment, expecting some further explanation. Delia remained silent and Kathryn said at last,

'Aren't you being rather ridiculous, Delia? You're in no position to prevent our marriage.'

'No?' Even that softly spoken word held a threat and Kathryn waited breathlessly for Delia to continue. 'John knows quite a lot about you—for example he knows you deliberately ingratiated yourself with Mr Southon. He also knows you're grasping and greedy, that you used your own methods of persuading an old man to part with treasures that should never have been taken out of the collection—'

'Persuade! How dare you suggest I persuaded him? I never so much as hinted that I wanted those presents!'

'John knows differently. But there's a great deal he doesn't know about you—things that I can tell him, Kathryn.' Her narrowed gaze became fixed significantly on Kathryn's face. 'And if you don't agree to give him up, then I shall most certainly let him know exactly what kind of a girl you really are.'

'I think you must be mad.' The disdain returned to Kathryn's eyes. 'There's absolutely nothing you can tell John about me—or rather, about my character, as you are obviously insinuating.'

'Oh, but there is,' returned Delia with undisguised triumph. 'For instance, will you deny that you know those moors extremely well?'

'I do know them well; yes, I know them very well.' Kathryn stared in some bewilderment. 'What has that to do with it?'

'You know them well . . . and yet you got lost?' The low and hateful tones revealed far more than the words and Kathryn actually stared in amazement.

'You think . . .?' She shook her head in a dazed sort of fashion, 'You can't think I—I did it deliberately —oh, you're hateful!' She quivered with anger and for a second or two this anger blocked her throat. 'The fog was dense; we couldn't see a hand in front of us. Anyone would get lost in that, no matter how well they knew the moors!'

'But anyone who knew the moors wouldn't have been so far from civilization at that time of the day—not in the month of October. You knew that if the fog came down you'd have difficulty, and yet you took no precautions?' A sneer of satisfaction curved her lips at Kathryn's rather frightened expression. 'John hasn't thought about this,' she went on insidiously. 'But then he wouldn't . . . unless someone brought it to his notice.'

'John w-would never believe you,' Kathryn faltered. 'Why, we could have died up there, had the fog persisted!'

'Rubbish! A search party would have been sent out. No one ever dies simply from being lost in the fog!'

'He won't believe you,' Kathryn whispered again, shaking her head weakly. 'I know he won't.'

'You don't sound too sure, for all that,' Delia sneered. 'However, Kathryn, we'll see whether or not he believes it.' Rising, she picked up her bag and gloves. 'There are other things he might like to know about you,' she added, still in that sneering, triumphant tone. 'I should give him up, Kathryn, if I were you—before *he* decides to give *you* up!' She put on her gloves, slowly, pressing out each crease in the soft, expensive kid. 'Incidentally, John knew you hated the idea of leaving here; you proved that to him by your insistence on his conforming to the terms of Mr Southon's will. So the knowledge that you'd go to any lengths to remain here won't altogether come as a surprise, will it?' And with that parting shot she moved to the door; a moment later it closed softly behind her.

Going to the window, Kathryn watched her get into the car and drive away. Then, turning, she walked slowly to the fire and stood gazing down into the glowing coals. John knew she was grasping and greedy, Delia had said; he knew she had persuaded Mr Southon to part with items from the Marbeck collection. Kathryn's mouth trembled convulsively and in spite of herself tears started to her eyes. These spiteful words of Delia's proved without doubt that John had talked about her, had said disparaging things in regard to her relationship with Mr Southon. He must have disliked her intensely to have discussed her in this way, must have despised her for accepting gifts which, in his opinion, belonged to the estate rather than to Mr Southon personally.

In spite of the contention that had existed between them as a result of that first disastrous meeting, Kathryn had always admired and respected John; never would she have believed him capable of discussing her—or any of his employees—in this way. The knowledge that he had done so weakened him in her eyes. He should have been above such petty spite, should have kept his conclusions regarding her character to himself.

Crushing down her disappointment at this discovery of a flaw in him, she dwelt a little fearfully on certain allusions Delia had made. 'There are other things he might like to know about you', she had said. Kathryn frowned through the tears that still lingered in her eyes. What things? There was nothing Delia could say that could in any way blacken her in John's eyes— In any case, Kathryn thought dejectedly, if Delia were to carry out her threat about bringing to John's notice the fact that Kathryn knew the moors, and should have known better than stay up there, then anything else she might find to say would surely fade into insignificance! If John really did believe her, the engagement would instantly be at an end.

Would he believe Delia? Perhaps. Kathryn could only wait and see.

CHAPTER VII

At the beginning of the following week John announced his intention of giving a party. Surprised, Kathryn asked him what it was for. He glanced down at her from his great height and although his blue eyes twinkled there was a hint of reproach in their depths which brought a puzzled frown to Kathryn's wide brow.

'According to my sister there are two dates a man should never forget or ignore—his wedding day and his wife's birthday. Why didn't you tell me you had a birthday coming on Wednesday?'

'You have a sister?' she asked, ignoring his question. 'But you never said. I'd begun to take it for granted you had no relatives.' Of course, she reflected, there had been no necessity for him to tell her about his family. Until very recently she had been of no more importance to him than Emily or Burrows, and it was hardly likely he would tell them about his affairs. 'How old is your sister?'

'Susan's twenty-six; she's the married one—the one who warned me to remember those two dates—or end up a deserted husband!'

'I'll never go quite that far,' she laughed, entering into his mood. 'Tell me about your family, John. You've obviously another sister. What's her name?'

'Felicity; she's just twenty, and engaged. Then I have a brother, Earl, also engaged.'

'And your parents?' How odd, she mused, to be asking these questions of the man to whom she was shortly to be married.

'My parents are in Ohio; that's where my home is. We're farmers—as you've already heard,' he added with a hint of amusement. He had said they must forget that first meeting, but such was his present mood that Kathryn ventured to say,

'Not merely small farmers, apparently.'

He shook his head.

'My great-grandfather went over from England and started farming in a fairly small way, but gradually he acquired more land—it was easy at that time, as you probably know—and now we do have many thousands of acres, mainly under wheat and maize.'

'Maize? What do you use that for?'

'Fattening cattle.' He paused and added, 'The canning factories are something over there. The cattle go in at one end and out of the other end comes not only the canned meat, lard and the rest, but fertilizers, leather, and—oh, numerous other commodities. Nothing's wasted.'

Kathryn frowned. She felt rather revolted at the idea of live creatures going in at one end of a factory and all these products coming out at the other. But she passed that off and asked about his parents again.

'How old are they? What are they like? Will they be pleased that you're marrying an English girl?'

'Which question would you like answered first?' he inquired with a quizzical lift of his brow. Kathryn blushed adorably; saw his eyes kindle with a strange light and lowered her head, saying,

'How old are they?'

'Mother's fifty-two and Father's a year older.' He smiled at her on suddenly reading her thoughts. 'I'm thirty-one in two months' time.'

'I thought you were about that age.' She then went

on to ask again whether his parents would welcome the fact of his marrying an English girl.

'They'll be delighted . . . so long as I'm happy.' The slight hesitation, the steadfast gaze he settled upon her. . . . Kathryn's heart leapt. Was he, like her, desiring to make a complete success of this marriage?

'I hope you'll be happy, John,' she returned seriously. 'I—I shall try my best. . . .'

'We'll both try, I'm thinking, as we're sensible people. Life could be most unpleasant were we to discover we'd made a mistake. However, you've promised to try, and—' He took her hand, holding it in a firm grip which reminded her of the night up on the moors when she had known the comfort of his strong hand clasping hers, keeping her close in the darkness and the fog. 'I shall try too, Kathryn. This promise I make you—solemnly.'

She looked up, her eyes bright with emotion. A great joy filled her as she saw his expression; her lips parted in unconscious invitation and in the intimacy of the moment John bent and kissed her, gently, without love or passion, and yet she sensed a promise of something more—a promise of sweet fulfilment, later, when time had given them the opportunity of adjustment.

'You haven't answered my question,' he remarked, releasing her hand. 'Why didn't you tell me you had a birthday coming?'

His words brought back the announcement that they were having a party and, flushing with pleasure in spite of her bewilderment, Kathryn asked how he had come to know about her birthday.

'I happened to be going through some of Mr Southon's papers and found a list of dates headed " Birthdays "; your name was included.'

'Oh. . . .' She watched his expression, recalling Delia's assertion that he had considered her greedy and grasping for accepting the presents Mr Southon had offered her. How could John say a thing like that? He looked at her most oddly, almost as if he were reading her thoughts. Suddenly Kathryn could not believe he would ever have talked about her in the way described by Delia and on impulse she said,

'John, did you ever say anything to anybody about my accepting gifts from Mr Southon?'

'Say anything?' he frowned. 'I don't think I understand, Kathryn. To whom would I be talking about such things?' He seemed a trifle angry and Kathryn half wished she had remained silent. But, her desire to know the truth being stronger than her fear of his change of mood, she persisted,

'You might have mentioned it—er—some time. I think you did wonder about my accepting gifts like the silver brushes, for instance, and you could have mentioned it to someone.'

Her first reaction was one of overwhelming relief. John had not talked about her. Delia had invented the whole thing. Kathryn recalled the incident when, on Delia's picking up one of her silver brushes, John had in fact made some remark about her, Kathryn, receiving many privileges from Mr Southon. That would naturally have registered with Delia—and she had used it to make Kathryn believe John had openly discussed her! How spiteful! How could anyone go to such lengths? But Delia would go further than that, Kathryn decided, and made a mental vow always to be on her guard.

Aware of John's eyes on her, Kathryn glanced up. No doubting his anger now and she instinctively shrank back, profoundly aware for the first time that John could, if he were driven, actually be cruel. It was an astonishing revelation, and a frightening one. Until now his attitude was ever one of superiority, cool, aloof and without any outward sign of a passionate nature within. But now Kathryn acknowledged the warning and resolved to take care, for John's anger could have most unpleasant consequences for the one foolish enough to arouse it.

'And who,' he icily inquired, 'would the "someone" be, to whom you anonymously refer?'

'No—no one in particular, John,' she replied in tones meant to pacify. 'It was just an idea, that's all.'

He looked amazed.

'An idea? You expect me to believe that? Who is this person with whom I could have been discussing you? Tell me—at once!'

But she shook her head, beginning to tremble as his face darkened with suppressed anger.

'There isn't anyone in particular—'

'Answer me, Kathryn. There must be some reason for your question. Why should you assume I'd been in the habit of talking about you in such a disgusting manner? I demand to know why you asked the question.'

Kathryn swallowed hard, fervently wishing she had held her tongue.

'Please don't worry about it,' she began, when he interrupted her.

'Kathryn,' he said softly, 'answer my question.'

She bit her lip, wondering how to frame her words.

'It was just an idea, as I told you. But I thought you might have said something to—to—Delia, for instance.'

An awful silence followed her words. Kathryn had experienced many uncomfortable moments since the coming of John Hyland, but apart from that first meeting none had been quite so uncomfortable as this. Was this fear owing to the fact that they were engaged? If that were the case, what effect was his displeasure going to have on her after she had become his wife?

'You actually believe I'd discuss you with another woman?—with Delia?' he asked harshly. 'Kindly explain yourself, Kathryn!'

'John . . . don't heed it,' she quivered. 'It isn't important—'

'How could you possibly have gained that impression? There must be some foundation for it!' he cut in wrathfully. 'I'll have your explanation, if you please!' Kathryn took an involuntary step backwards, an action that only served to add fuel to the flame of his wrath.

'I—we—that is, Delia and I were talking, and it seemed as if you'd—I mean, I had the impression that you might just have made some remark—' A hand was raised in a light and airy gesture. 'I'm mistaken, obviously,' she added, even managing a rather cracked little laugh. 'Forget it, John; it's nothing—nothing at all.'

He continued to stare down at her, his eyes slowly narrowing, and with a little gulp of apprehension Kathryn wondered if he would pursue the matter further, would insist on having the truth. But to her profound relief he merely shrugged and within seconds his face had cleared and all anger had left him. Nevertheless, he wasn't satisfied, and Kathryn had the uncomfortable conviction that he would eventually demand a fully explanation.

However, for the present he appeared to be satisfied with her answer and for the next half hour or so they discussed Kathryn's birthday party.

'I suppose you'll be wanting to ask your sisters?' His lips pursed and she found herself blushing, for he must be remembering that rowdy scene, and that dreadful room of Rita's.

'They can behave,' she submitted. 'I'd like them to come.'

'Certainly they shall come,' he responded swiftly. 'You must ask whom you like, Kathryn. It's your party.'

The list was made out; Kathryn had two friends whom she wished to ask, and her father and mother. Then she mentioned Michael, watching John's face as she did so.

His expression told her nothing as he agreed that Michael be invited.

'And that's all,' Kathryn said. 'It won't be a very big party unless you invite someone, John.'

'I did think of the Slades. You get on very well with them, I've noticed.' Was he being tactful, or could he be in ignorance of the hostility existing between Delia and herself? As for Mr and Mrs Slade, he was quite right about them. Kathryn had always liked them and in Mr Southon's day they had treated her with the utmost kindness and consideration, regarding her more in the light of a daughter of the house than an employee.

'Yes, we'll ask the Slades,' she agreed, noticing his questioning gaze at her hesitation. She could keep away from Delia, Kathryn thought, wondering if, perhaps, she would decline the invitation. However, all the invitations were accepted; the guests including the two school friends of Kathryn's and a young married couple who lived at the Old Smithy, a charming Tudor house set on a hill overlooking the tree-lined lane and the ancient church. Andrea Martin had been friendly with Kathryn ever since she and her husband had come to the village three years ago on their marriage; and when John arrived at the Hall both she and Bernard had called, being introduced to John by Kathryn. Bernard and John had taken to each other on sight, and it now seemed that a close friendship between the two couples would swiftly develop.

The great Dining Room was lighted by candles only. They were in ornate silver candlesticks and set amid lovely floral decorations which were displayed right down the centre of the lovely sixteenth-century refectory table.

'Don't you feel important, Kate?' Dawn was seated on one side of her and she laughed as she asked the question. 'I never thought to be sitting here as a guest of my sister. I think I'll have to reform and act as the sister of the lady of the manor should.'

'You don't need to reform,' Kathryn quickly replied.
'All you need do is settle down.'

'Get married, you mean?'

'Not necessarily, but quieten down, that's what I
really meant.'

'You mean become old-fashioned and staid like you?'
Dawn paused in thought. 'Well . . . if this is where
staidness gets you, I don't think it's a bad idea after all.
Yes,' she nodded, 'I might take your advice at that.'
Kathryn laughed, and caught her fiancé's eye. He
smiled at her and her heart fluttered with sudden joy.
The past six years at Marbeck Hall had been years of
quiet pleasure, and a continuance of this was all she had
hoped for when, after Mr Southon's death, a new heir
was traced, so far away across the Atlantic. Yes, she
had hoped with all her heart that this John Hyland
would keep her in his employ, allowing her to go on
living there, in that state of quiet pleasure. . . . But
this, this was sheer wonderment, not only because she
would be here for the rest of her days but, much more
important, because she would be John's wife. Her quiet
pleasure had turned to excitement bordering on ecstasy.
John's smile deepened, and Kathryn knew it was owing
to the blush that had suddenly tinted her cheeks. She
looked down at her plate, and spent the next few minutes
concentrating on her food.

The meal over, they all went into the Drawing Room,
and it was only then that Kathryn and Michael found an
opportunity to talk. Michael, Kathryn knew, had
bought some rare Sèvres porcelain and she began to ask
him about it. But he was not interested in antiques,
strangely, and his usual bright smile was absent as, sitting down beside her on the couch, he asked her if she
were happy.

'Yes, Michael, I'm happy,' she replied truthfully.
Her eyes were on Delia, who was sitting at the other side

of the room talking to Andrea and Bernard. She was smiling in her charming way, but suddenly sensing Kathryn's eyes upon her, she lifted her face; the smile faded, and its place taken by an expression of sheer hatred. Kathryn started visibly and Michael followed the direction of her gaze.

'You'll have trouble with her,' he declared, for the moment diverted from what he had intended saying. 'She was all set to becoming mistress of Marbeck; it's a coveted position you have, Kathryn.' She felt uncomfortable. Did everyone believe what Michael had so subtly hinted—that she was lucky only because of the position she would hold?—because of living in this, the most beautiful and famous house in the whole of Cheshire? Returning his gaze to Kathryn, Michael's eyes became clouded and anxious. 'I suppose this isn't the time to bring it up,' he said, 'but you know how I feel about you? I asked you to marry me—' He broke off awkwardly and Kathryn glanced down at her hands, hiding her embarrassment.

'I wasn't in love with you, Michael,' she submitted in rather gentle tones.

'Are you in love with John Hyland?' he countered bluntly, and she swiftly raised her head.

'Why should you ask that?'

'Simply because you've never got along all that well.' A difficult pause and then, 'Was this engagement the result of what happened on the moors—or had you both decided to marry before then?'

'I can't answer that.' She glanced at him indignantly. 'You shouldn't ask these pertinent questions, Michael.'

He shrugged.

'I agree—but the engagement was so sudden. You were all set for leaving here at the end of the year, and, it appeared, John was all set to marry Delia Slade.'

In spite of her protest of a moment ago she had to

ask, on a note of deep concern,

'Are people thinking our engagement's the result of what happened on the moors?' If so, she thought, then John's manoeuvre was not to be effective after all.

'Not that I know of. Most people seem to think it was to be announced anyway. Was it, Kathryn?'

'No,' she admitted. 'But that's all I can say, Michael. Please let this matter drop.'

'I love you, Kathryn,' he began, but she shook her head.

'We've a good deal in common; we love the same things, but that's all.' She looked at him squarely and, as she had half expected, he could not meet her gaze. 'You haven't found the right one yet, Michael,' she smiled. 'You'll be in no doubt at all when she does eventually come along.' The happiness in her voice impressed itself upon him and he did look at her then, eyeing her in some amazement.

'You *do* love him?' he said wonderingly.

'Yes, Michael, I love him,' she returned simply, adding, with a little self-conscious laugh, 'I think I've known it for some time.'

'And he—does he love you?'

'We're engaged,' she exclaimed, managing to laugh. 'Of course he loves me!'

A few minutes later Dawn and Rita came over and Kathryn introduced them to Michael. They all sat talking for some time and then Kathryn went over to her parents. They had been chatting to John and Mrs Ramsey's face was fairly glowing when she looked up at her daughter.

'We do like your John,' she exclaimed impulsively. 'He's nice, Kathryn, and I think you'll both do very well, in spite of the reason for your marrying.'

Kathryn smiled, and glanced at her father; his eyes twinkled as, moving to one side of the couch, he made room for Kathryn to sit between them.

'When's the wedding to take place?' he asked, glancing proudly at her. She was dressed in turquoise velvet and wore the lovely diamond necklace John had given her for her birthday. Her hair, falling like a shower of gold on to her shoulders, was held off her face with a diamond and ruby stud, matching the ring on her finger. 'John doesn't appear to be the sort of man who will want any unnecessary delay.'

'We haven't discussed the date,' she said, her eyes straying to where John was standing by the beautiful William and Mary bureau. Delia was beside him and they appeared to be deeply engrossed in a discussion on the Zuccaro portrait which hung alongside the bureau. It was the portrait of Lady Anne Fitton, with her children Edward and Mary, the portrait which Kathryn had particularly pointed out to John on that first evening when, at his request, she had taken him over the house.

'We can probably expect it to be fixed soon after the house is closed for the winter.' Mrs Ramsey's eager and expectant tones broke into Kathryn's musings and she turned, puzzled.

'Fixed?'

'The date for the wedding,' her father interposed, a grin suddenly creasing his face. 'Mother's in a hurry.'

'No such thing!' she retorted, flushing. 'But there's no sense in waiting.' Kathryn turned to look at her. Was her mother afraid something would occur to prevent the marriage? She appeared happy enough, but Kathryn sensed this underlying anxiety. Kathryn's gaze returned to John and his lovely companion and a tinge of fear took the happiness from her eyes. Was it the picture they were discussing? Or could Delia possibly be telling John—?

But no, even Delia would not be so malicious as that. Her words were merely an idle threat, uttered in the heat of the moment and stemming from her quite understandable disappointment at the idea of John's marrying someone else. Making a determined effort to crush down her apprehension Kathryn turned her attention to her parents.

'We're supposed to be having dancing,' she told them, looking at the clock. 'John's engaged a small orchestra from Macclesfield, but it hasn't arrived yet. I wonder what's happened?'

But within a few minutes Burrows was informing John that the orchestra was here and a little while later the dance was in progress in the Long Hall, from where most of the furniture had been removed.

'Who's that girl making eyes at your bloke?' Rita wanted to know as, rather breathless, she flopped down beside Kathryn on the wide, plush-covered seat that had been placed along one wall. 'I seem to remember seeing her here before he came. Is she a friend of his?'

Following the direction of her sister's gaze, Kathryn watched her fiancé dancing with Delia. He held her much too close, Kathryn decided, wondering whether the odd little sensation that assailed her was the result of hurt—or jealousy. Perhaps something of both, she thought, conscious of a return of that fear which she had so determinedly endeavoured to throw off.

'She is a friend, yes.'

'Well, I'd have something to say if she looked at my fiancé like that! What nerve—and with everyone watching too. She's downright brazen, Kate! And what's she saying to him, with her face so close to his ear?'

'You have to get close—with the band playing,' Kathryn said reasonably. 'I don't suppose it's anything important.'

Michael came to her and she got up with him; then she danced with her father. John came later and smilingly took her hand, urging her to her feet with a noticeably proprietorial gesture. He held her just as close as he had held Delia—closer in fact, for at one time his head was bent so that his cheek lightly touched hers.

'You look very beautiful tonight, Kathryn,' he murmured softly. 'I'm proud of you, my dear.'

All her fears vanished and she thought her heartbeats would surely reveal more than her lips would have dared to tell. Suddenly the pressure of John's arm tightened as he swung her out, avoiding a collision with Bernard and Delia. Bernard threw them a good-humoured smile, but, catching Delia's eye, Kathryn gave a start. Never had she seen such venom in a glance, and all at once she heard again Michael's declaration that she would have trouble with Delia. Involuntarily she shuddered and John held her away.

'What was that for? You can't be cold.' He sounded anxious, and Kathryn sent him a reassuring smile.

'It was nothing,' she murmured, but her fingers moved convulsively in his, as if she sought comfort from his touch.

The buffet was set out in the Dining Room, on the great oak table, and when the music stopped John and Kathryn went for some refreshments, joining Mr and Mrs Slade, who were sitting at one of the small tables by the wall.

'You look very happy tonight,' Mr Slade remarked, his eyes straying appreciatively over Kathryn. 'And very pretty, if I might say so.'

'Thank you.' Kathryn spoke demurely, aware of the hint of colour rising in her face.

'Yes—turquoise suits you,' his wife added, but although her comment was sincere, as was her smile, Kathryn sensed her bitter disappointment at the way things had turned out.

John had gone for the refreshments, and he returned carrying two plates containing a variety of snacks.

'I didn't know what you wanted,' he said, putting a plate down in front of Kathryn. 'Is that all right?'

'Yes, thank you, John.'

After a little while the older couple left them, but

almost at once Delia came from the Long Hall and sat down at their table.

'I'll get you something,' John offered graciously, rising. 'What would you like? The same as we have?'

'Yes, please, John. It looks very appetizing.' Her lovely lashes fluttered and, glancing up at her fiancé, Kathryn saw a muscle move in his throat, as if he were swallowing something hard there. She frowned, recalling, against her will, Delia's assertion that John was making a sacrifice by offering to marry Kathryn.

No sooner had he moved away than Delia looked across at Kathryn and whispered vehemently,

'Quite the experienced hostess, aren't you, Kathryn?'

'I wouldn't say I was experienced.' Kathryn swivelled round, watching John's tall figure moving towards the refectory table.

'Give him up,' snapped Delia, watching her. 'I've told you you'll never marry him, so you'll save yourself a good deal of humiliation if you take my advice without further delay.'

'Your advice, Delia, sounds more like an order.' Kathryn was trembling inwardly, although her voice was cool, and even held a small note of hauteur in its depths.

'Very well, it's an order!' Delia's eyes were narrowed, and her mouth was twisted in an ugly line. 'I've warned you, Kathryn, if you don't give him up, then he'll throw you over, because I meant what I said about opening his eyes to what you really are.'

Fear touched Kathryn again, but as she stopped to consider Delia's threat she began to realize her fears were stupid. For even if Delia were inclined to reveal her suspicions to John, what form of approach could she make? She could scarcely turn to him and say, baldly, that Kathryn had deliberately trapped him into marriage. No, Kathryn felt sure she had nothing to fear, nothing at all.

'I'm not afraid of you.' Kathryn gave a little toss of

her head and Delia's mouth took on a tight and almost cruel line. 'There's no way you can tell him. I've thought about it carefully, and you couldn't even begin to broach such a subject. You're bluffing, Delia, and I'm calling your bluff!'

'You—!' The dark eyes became embers of hate. Her glance flicked past Kathryn; John was returning, with the plate of refreshments in his hand. 'Calling my bluff, are you?' she hissed. 'Very well, if that's your last word—' She broke off, and the change was miraculous. Her lips became full and adorably inviting; her eyes were wide and softly feminine; her silken lashes fluttered in the most enchanting way. A smile from John brought her lovely mouth curving in swift response. Kathryn gasped audibly; John cocked an eyebrow questioningly, but Delia spoke before either he or Kathryn could do so.

'Thank you John— Oh, my head! I feel quite dizzy.'

'You're ill?' John's brow knit in concern. 'What is it, Delia?'

'My head—oh, it's spinning.' She put a trembling hand to her brow. 'I didn't say anything to anyone, but I slipped and fell just before I came out, and banged my head against the corner of the wardrobe. I went dizzy then, but it passed off and I thought no more about it.'

'But you should have,' John said sternly. 'Where did you bang it?'

'On the back. . . .' Her hand moved and she winced. 'The dizziness will go in a minute; it can't be anything serious.' She looked up appealingly at John. 'Could I have a glass of water?'

'Of course; I'll get you one. Kathryn, fetch Mr and Mrs Slade—'

'No—' Delia shook her head, then winced again. 'No, please don't mention this to them—they'll worry so and—and I'm sure it will pass in a moment or two.'

'But we ought to fetch your parents,' Kathryn protested. 'If you feel so ill.'

'I'll be all right,' insisted Delia. 'If I could have that water?'

John went out to get it; Kathryn examined Delia's face anxiously, expecting it to have lost some of its colour. This was not so, but Delia was trembling visibly.

'Do you feel very bad?' Kathryn asked, rising. 'Can I do anything for you?'

'I'd like to lie down . . . perhaps in the small sitting-room? It'll be quiet there—and the guests won't know anything about this.'

'Yes, that's a good idea. You can lie down on the couch by the fire.'

John fetched the water and Delia sipped it; the hand that held it still trembled.

'I think you ought to go home,' John began, when Kathryn interrupted him.

'Delia wants to be quiet, so she's going to lie down on the couch in the sitting-room for a while. Will you help her, John?'

'Don't say a word about this to my parents,' begged Delia again as, a few minutes later, she lay on the couch, her head propped against the cushions Kathryn had arranged for her. 'They'd be so anxious—and Father's heart's not too good; any shock might be dangerous. Promise you'll not tell them?'

'Very well,' John agreed, although after some considerable hesitation. 'I'd much rather bring them in here, but if your father's heart's weak then perhaps we'd better keep silent.'

'I feel awful—' Delia looked apologetically at Kathryn. 'I'm keeping you from your guests.'

'That's all right, Delia. It can't be helped, if you're ill.'

'But both of you—look, please go back; I'll be all
136

right here by myself.'

'We're not leaving you,' declared Kathryn firmly.
'John, perhaps you'd like to go—?'

'But it's your party, Kathryn,' interrupted Delia.
'Please go in to them. I'll feel so guilty if you won't.'

Kathryn looked uncertainly at John, who nodded.

'Perhaps you should. I'll stay with Delia—for a
while at any rate. You can come back in about twenty
minutes or so, if you wish.'

'I'll probably be better by then,' Delia said hopefully,
trying to force a smile.

Kathryn went back to the Long Hall, and was just
getting up to dance with Bernard when she heard Andrea
say to Mrs Slade,

'Is Delia ill? I saw John and Kathryn helping her
along the corridor—'

'Excuse me, Bernard,' Kathryn said swiftly. 'I'll be
with you in a minute.' And, leaving him to stare in
puzzlement after her, she almost ran back to the sitting-
room, intending to warn Delia.

The door was ajar; Kathryn pushed it open . . . and
stood just inside the room. Delia's eyes were closed; she
sounded as if she were rambling—she *was* rambling,
Kathryn realized, after listening a moment longer.

'It's not a very nice thing to say, Kathryn, that his
claim was—was weak . . . that it's a pity Mr Southon
never married . . . what? He's marrying you to save
his own face?—and not because he's thinking about you
at all? How can you say such things?—and after you've
admitted you know those moors . . . that you knew you
should have come away earlier . . . only you—you stayed
on purpose. . . . Oh, my head!' A small silence and
then, 'You deliberately set out to compromise him? I'd
no idea . . . when you said you'd go to any lengths to
stay. . . .'

White to the lips, Kathryn at last managed to come
further into the room. John was standing by the couch,

his profile drawn and harsh, his hands clenched by his sides.

'Mrs Slade knows Delia's ill. Andrea saw us helping her along the corridor.' Kathryn was amazed she could speak at all, and much more that she could be so calm. It was as if she were numbed by the astounding knowledge that Delia could go to these lengths. The scheme had been well thought out to the last detail—even to extracting from John the promise not to let her parents know of the attack. What would she do now? But her eyes were already fluttering open; she stared from John to Kathryn in a dazed and uncomprehending manner. Kathryn felt sick with disgust as she watched Delia 'come round'. It was all over in seconds. She sat up, passing a hand across her forehead.

'Have I dozed? I must have—and I feel much better for it.' She smiled at John and added, 'I'm fine now, I knew it would pass in no time at all!'

John turned and Kathryn lifted her eyes to meet his. Would he see through this girl? No; for not only was the scheme a clever one, but John, himself so honourable, would never so much as suspect Delia of such malevolent conduct. And in addition to this, John was totally unaware of the enmity existing between his fiancée and the girl who would in all probability have become his wife, had events taken their natural course.

With her fiancé's condemnation filling the room, and his eyes burning into her, Kathryn turned away. Words were useless, for John believed all he had heard.

CHAPTER VIII

Kathryn lay on the lovely French bed, looking up at the ornate ceiling. Was this the end? It must be, for John would never want to marry her after what he had heard, gossip or no gossip. She turned, glancing at the clock.

Sleep hadn't come to her at all, and although certain she could now have dozed she got up and, slipping on a housecoat, sat down at the dressing-table and began to brush her hair. The little jewelled stud lay on the tray, and from the ring stand hung one ring—her engagement ring. Should she return it at once? Perhaps that would save both John and herself much embarrassment. Better still, she could just quietly disappear—go back home, leaving John a note. Yes, that would be the best thing to do—and the most dignified.

How long would John wait before becoming engaged to Delia? Kathryn wondered. He would have to wait a little while, naturally, but Kathryn did not think he would delay for very long.

Should she go now, this morning, while John was still in bed? After a little consideration Kathryn decided against that course; it savoured too much of the melodramatic. Moreover, the very action would appear to prove her guilt. She would go down to breakfast; she would face him unflinchingly. With this decision firmly made, she had her bath, dressed herself, and went downstairs. John was not yet up and she went out, wandering in the grounds. The nip of autumn sharpened the air and a faint mist hung above the tallest trees. The only sounds were those made by the waterfowl on the lakes. Kathryn walked about for over an hour, but when she returned to the house there was still no sign of John. She went into the breakfast room. Her eyes scanned the table; he had eaten—eaten alone, something he had not done since their engagement. Breakfast had been a cosy, intimate meal which they had begun to take together, and to which Kathryn eagerly looked forward. She had believed John enjoyed it just as much—in fact, she knew he had . . . until now.

The dishes were still on the sideboard, but even the sight of food would have made Kathryn feel ill and she rang for Emily, telling her to remove the breakfast as she wasn't hungry.

'Mr Hyland left a message for you,' Emily said, looking a little oddly at Kathryn. 'He's going into Manchester on business and won't be back until late. I understand he won't be back for dinner.'

'Thank you, Emily.'

'Your breakfast, Miss Ramsey—are you not well?'

'Quite well, thank you, Emily,' she smiled. 'I just don't feel hungry, that's all.'

Had John done this deliberately—in order to give her the opportunity of packing up her belongings and leaving the Hall? It seemed like it, as he had made no mention yesterday of any business he had to conduct in Manchester. Well, she would go, for that was obviously what he wanted.

'But he could have spoken to me about it,' she whispered convulsively, five minutes later when, her suitcase open on the bed, she was preparing to pack. He could even have asked if I had any explanation to offer.' Which is what would naturally have occurred had the engagement been a normal one, had they been marrying for love. With love all misunderstandings could usually be resolved.

Try as she would, Kathryn could not get on with her packing. She had no heart in it, even though her determination to leave today was still very strong. At last, with all her things scattered about on the bed, and even on the floor, she stopped and, sitting down, wrote the note she intended leaving for John. It was short, stating that, in view of what he had heard from Delia, he would no longer wish to continue with the engagement. Kathryn ended with, 'I'm leaving all the presents Mr Southon gave me, also my ring and my birthday gift from you.'

The interruption did not have the desired effect, and even when the letter was written Kathryn still had no heart to continue with her packing. At last she left it, but as Emily had not yet been in to tidy the room, Kathryn locked the door. The servants would know soon enough; there was no sense in allowing them to see anything yet.

What should she do? For the first time since coming to Marbeck she was at a loose end. Normally she would clean some of the silver, or wash the china, or perform some other labour of love, but she had no more enthusiasm for any of this than she had for her packing.

Michael. . . . He had bought that Sèvres porcelain, and during their conversation last evening he had expressed the wish that she would come along to his shop and look at it. It would be a heaven-sent diversion; she could take one of the cars, and be back in plenty of time to pack and be gone before John's return.

She rang Michael, telling him to expect her; he was delighted but puzzled.

'Are you a lady of leisure already? I thought you were still working for Mr Hyland, even though you're engaged.'

The words came as a shock. Yes, she was still employed by John. She ought not by rights to leave him without notice, she realized with a bitter curve of her lips. But he would scarcely expect that—or desire it, even though her departure would undoubtedly inconvenience him, especially as the house was not to be closed for another three weeks.

Michael was in the shop, dusting some weapons he had just bought. After greeting her with a smile he held out one of the weapons.

'What do you think of this?' It was a blunderbuss, and in very fine condition.

'It's lovely.' She handled it, examining it carefully. 'You've paid a lot for it, Michael.' It was a statement, but to her surprise he shook his head.

'A man brought it in this morning and asked what I'd give.'

'He didn't know the value?'

'Hadn't a clue. His grandmother had died and this was in the attic—all covered with dust and cobwebs. The man was going to throw it out, but someone told him I was advertising for weapons. I got it for a couple of quid.'

'Michael,' she gasped. 'How could you!'

'Business, Kathryn,' he laughed, adding, 'Perhaps it's a good thing you didn't consent to marry me after all. I've an idea you'd be no good in business.'

'I'd have to pay what an article was worth,' she agreed. 'I'd feel dreadfully guilty if I didn't.'

'Then you'd neither make money nor have the thrill of finding a bargain. This fellow's delighted—only too relieved that he didn't throw it in the dustbin.' He laughed again at her expression. 'This sort of thing's happening all the time. If everybody knew everything then we'd have to go out of business.' Kathryn returned the blunderbuss to him and he put it in the window. 'Come in the back; we'll have some coffee and then I'll show you the Sèvres.'

'Were they a bargain?' she asked.

'I'm satisfied, shall we say? But I didn't get them cheap—for of course they're marked and people know what they are.'

It was as they were drinking their coffee that Michael suddenly realized Kathryn was not her usual bright self. She saw his expression change as he examined her face and was quite prepared when at last he said anxiously,

'Are you not very well, Kathryn?'

'I'm well, yes, thank you, Michael.'

'But something's wrong, obviously. It's not John?'

She swallowed; Michael would have to know, very soon, for the broken engagement would be front page news just as the engagement itself had been. But although he was a good friend she felt strangely disinclined to confide in him. So all she said was,

'It isn't John exactly. But I've decided I'm not a suitable wife for him and I'm leaving him. I'm breaking the engagement.'

A small silence followed this announcement; Michael looked at her searchingly and then, putting down his cup, he leant forward in his chair.

'You're not the girl to get engaged one week and break it off the next. What's up, Kathryn?'

She flushed, wondering how to rectify the impression she had given him. But there was no rectifying it, for he was too intelligent a person to be fobbed off with some weak equivocation on her part. Resignedly she shrugged, and told him the whole truth.

'The bitch!' he exclaimed, in a voice she never thought to hear from him. For Michael was of a quiet, serious disposition, wholly absorbed in his work, which was also his hobby. He was a man not easily ruffled and, until now, Kathryn had never suspected him of any violent emotions whatsoever. But there was no doubt of his fury and, for some quite incomprehensible reason, Kathryn found his anger against Delia strangely comforting. It were as if she had an ally, after fighting alone, with John and Delia ranged against her. That this was not strictly true, she freely owned, but, as she naturally felt a little sorry for herself, the idea had persisted from the moment when, looking up into her fiancé's face, Kathryn knew that he believed everything Delia had said when supposedly rambling. 'The rotten, scheming bitch! And John believes it all, you say? Why didn't you defend yourself, you idiot?'

Kathryn spread her hands.

'What could I say? I saw at once that he believed her, and so I went back to the guests. When they'd all gone I went straight up to my room. I couldn't have spoken to him last night, Michael; I felt too sick and disgusted, for I never thought she'd go that far. And besides, it was my birthday and I'd had a lovely time.'

I couldn't face a scene after that—' She shook her head vigorously. 'No, it would have been too awful.'

' But this morning? You've talked about it, surely?'

' I haven't seen John this morning,' she quivered and, as he stared at her in surprised inquiry, she went on to explain how she and John had missed each other.

' He didn't ask for you—send one of the maids out for you?'

' Perhaps he didn't know I was outside,' she returned. ' He might have concluded I was still in bed.'

Michael's anger had subsided as swiftly as it had arisen. He was thinking and appeared not to have absorbed Kathryn's last words.

' So I was right in surmising the engagement resulted from your being together on the moors all night,' he said musingly, and Kathryn flushed.

' I know I said John loved me,' she confessed, ' but I think it was more that I tried to deceive myself rather than you—because I wanted it so much.' She averted her head, half regretting that confidence, while at the same time sensitive of the fact that Michael was thoroughly reliable and she could be very sure that anything she said would be kept entirely to himself.

' You really love him, Kathryn?' he asked seriously, his eyes holding hers in a steady searching gaze.

' I love him, Michael, I don't know how I'm—I'm going to—to live without—without—' She looked across at him, her lovely eyes glistening with tears. ' Why did I have to meet him? I wish I never had!'

' Well, you have met him, and you're engaged to him,' Michael returned practically. ' And if you love him you'll fight for what you want.'

' Fight?' she queried hopelessly. ' I'm not fighting, Michael. I'm just getting out and leaving them to live their lives together.'

' You're not taking any steps at all to defend yourself?' he queried on a note of disbelief, and, when she

144

shook her head despairingly, 'You'd let her win? By heaven, Kathryn, I'd have expected you to have more mettle than that!'

'But what can I do?' she returned helplessly.

'You can fight, as I've just said. John hasn't asked you for his freedom, so why give it to him?'

'He hasn't yet, because we've not even spoken to one another since it happened. But he will ask me to release him; it's only natural.'

'I wonder. . . .' Michael spoke to himself and Kathryn gave a little start of surprise.

'There's no doubt about it,' she assured him swiftly. 'John can't possibly have any wish to marry me now.'

'I'm not so sure. He thought of the gossip before, and unless I'm very much mistaken he'll consider that again.'

'No, Michael, you're wrong. Remember that, before, he had nothing against me personally—well, nothing serious,' she added, recalling the disastrous start she had made with him. 'But now he has all this; my character's completely blackened in his eyes. I'm a scheming woman, according to Delia. John knew I desperately wanted to stay at the Hall, and so he'd readily believe I deliberately planned the whole thing up there on the moors—'

'Nonsense! Now I come to think of it, Kathryn, I'm not so sure at all that Delia's little ruse was all that convincing. How, for instance, could you have planned the whole thing when you didn't have any idea about the fog?'

'No, but as the fog did come, I should have been cautious and advised John to leave. It *looks* as if I took advantage of the situation to compromise John. It does, Michael, no matter what you say,' Kathryn added, shaking her head in a little gesture of conviction.

'These other things she's attributed to you—did you say them?'

' I did say John's claim to the estate was weak, but I didn't mean it in a nasty way; Delia's twisted it to suit her own ends.'

' And what about your saying John is marrying you to save his own face? Was that true?' he asked, and again Kathryn had to admit it was. ' You know, Kathryn,' said Michael admonishingly, ' you've been a very foolish girl. You've known for some time that Delia Slade's poison, and yet you said these things to her—things that could be twisted in this way. Forgive me for saying it, but you should have had more sense.'

' I did try to be on my guard.'

' She was too clever for you—you're not up to that sort of invidious behaviour.' The shop bell sounded and Michael left her for a moment. When he returned she was staring despondently into the fire. ' You're not giving in, Kathryn,' he stated almost angrily. ' You're going to follow your natural instinct and fight this damned woman.'

' Natural instinct?' she queried uncomprehendingly.

' To fight for what one wants is a natural instinct. Delia's fought, but hers are dirty ways and she's not hesitated to stab you in the back. However, you still possess the strongest weapon. You're engaged to John —and if you've an ounce of common sense you'll stay that way. For John Hyland might be deceived now, but he's no fool. Some day he's going to see through that one!'

' I can't insist on remaining engaged to him,' protested Kathryn impatiently. ' Life would be unbearable for us both.'

An exasperated sigh portrayed Michael's impatience, but his next words impressed themselves deeply upon her.

' You love him, and yet you'd condemn him to a life with a woman of Delia's character?'

' Condemn?'

146

'He'd find her out in no time at all. It's my bet that once married to him she wouldn't trouble to keep up that pose—she couldn't anyway. No one can live a lie for very long. At present he's safe from Delia, but were you to release him you could be condemning him to a life of misery.'

'I never thought of it like that.' She looked up, and suddenly her eyes glinted with the light of determination. 'I'll do as you say, Michael. I'll stay engaged to him for as long as I can—and I might even have an opportunity of letting John know what she's really like.'

'Good girl,' he applauded, giving her a broad smile. 'Something'll crop up. She'll give herself away one of these days, you can take my word for it.'

'Life will be pretty uncomfortable,' Kathryn put in. 'John can be—be very—' She broke off, unwilling to talk about John in this vein of disloyalty. Michael finished the sentence for her.

'Difficult, to say the least, eh?'

She nodded unhappily, but her determination remained and was even strengthened as, passing the entrance to the Slades' house on her way home, she was greeted with a sneer of triumph from Delia who, sitting at the wheel of her car, was waiting to turn out into the lane.

To Kathryn's surprise John was in when she arrived back at the Hall; his car was in the drive and Kathryn experienced a little sickening feeling in the pit of her stomach as she visualized the coming scene. After putting the car in the garage she entered the house, intending to go up to her room quietly, in order to compose herself and think out clearly the method with which she would handle the situation. She was half way up the stairs when he came from the Library and called to her. She turned, white-faced and trembling, her hand gripping the banister rail as if for support.

'I've been looking for you, Kathryn. Where have

you been?'

She cleared her throat nervously.

'I went to see Michael.'

'Michael?' he echoed sharply. 'You've spent the whole day with him?'

Kathryn glanced at the clock; it was a quarter past four.

'I stayed a long while, yes. We had lunch out and then went back to the shop—'

'You just took the day off?' His brows lifted; in her overwrought state Kathryn saw him again as the impersonal employer, arrogant and superior.

'I felt the need of company, John,' she returned in a voice scarcely above a whisper. 'You'd gone out and Emily said you wouldn't be back all day. She said you had business in Manchester.' Kathryn sent him a questioning glance which, to her surprise, he avoided.

'I was back earlier than I expected,' was all the information she received about that, but he went on to say he wanted to speak to her, and would be in the small sitting-room when she came down. 'Don't be too long,' he said, and went back into the Library.

What did he want to say? He meant to break the engagement, obviously.

Kathryn went upstairs, unlocked her door and entered the room. Perhaps a wash and change would give her confidence. Her eyes wandered round the room, noting the disorder, and then they came to rest on the letter, neatly folded, which lay on the silver tray. John had been looking for her. . . . Had he tried her door? It was more than likely, she concluded, and heaved a sigh of relief that he hadn't been able to get in, as he would obviously have read the note. Walking over to the dressing table, she took it up, scanning its contents and picking out bits here and there. ' —I saw by your face that you believed Delia, and so any denials on my part would be wasted; indeed, some of the things Delia said

148

I could not in all honesty refute . . . there have been many misunderstandings, and I know I'm to blame for them . . . were our engagement based on something stronger than necessity, perhaps I could explain . . . I'm leaving the presents. . . .' Slowly she folded the letter up and then, slipping it into a little Chinese pot-pourri jar, she replaced the lid on the jar and began hastily to put the room into some sort of order.

Ten minutes later, wearing her ring, she went down-stairs again. Might as well get the whole thing over and done with, she decided, although she did wonder how she would find the courage to defy him, should he tell her to go. *Should* he tell her? There was not much doubt about that!

It was an exceptionally dull day with low clouds hang-ing; the oak-beamed room was dark, but the glow from the fire sent a rosy light on to the walls, giving them an added warmth and softness. From a huge bowl of chrysanthemums in the corner a subtle perfume emanated to mingle with the slightly pungent smell of pine logs burning. John stood at one side of the chimneypiece, his arm resting along the mantelshelf. In the dim light his face looked incredibly hard and grim, but in the slight protrusion of his lower lip there lay the suggestion of an inner tenseness that seemed to detract from that first impression of harsh inflexibility. The idea was fleeting and as his eyes flickered over her Kathryn saw only cold contempt and bitter accusation. It would be easier to accept his decision, she thought, her courage threatening to desert her. But she would not leave him free to marry Delia, and so ruin his whole life! Her love was too strong to allow her to falter in her resolution. His blue eyes kindled; she felt instinctively that he was about to speak, to tell her to go, that he was finished with her for good. And she knew she must speak first, say what she meant to say before John could begin, otherwise her courage would fail and she would find herself meekly accepting his decision. And owing to her haste her voice sounded cracked and harsh, and her eyes flashed defiance at him.

'I know what you're going to say, John, but I'm having my say first. I'm engaged to you and I'll never give you your freedom! I know that after what you were told last night you must hate and despise me, but you've asked me to marry you and I'm not giving you up!' Ever afterwards she wondered just how she had managed to bring her words out, for she was trembling with fright. Could John see she was trembling? She didn't want him to know of her fear, because then he might browbeat her into submission to his will. But perhaps he would conclude that her trembling resulted from anger, she thought, watching him hopefully. 'I'll never give you up,' she went on, as if to strengthen the impression of anger and defiance. That should convince him she wasn't afraid. Nevertheless, she was tempted to add, just for good measure, 'And there isn't a thing you can do about it!'

'You—!' For a moment he looked more stunned than angry, and Kathryn stared at him with a mixture of bewilderment and surprise. But the expected outburst was merely being delayed; she saw that almost at once, for his eyes suddenly became frozen pools of wrath, and little white patches crept into his jaw. He took an involuntary step towards her and her heart thudded against her ribs. 'You'd stay here—force me to marry you even though, as you've just said, I hate and despise you?' His voice was vibrant with fury and Kathryn wondered why she made this effort to fight; he must defeat her . . . he must! She could not speak and he went on, his eyes raking her contemptuously, 'You'd hold me to my promise—after what I've learned?'

'I'll never give you up!' she retorted, with far more defiance than she felt.

Silence followed her words—the silence of incredulous

disbelief. And then his eyes bored into her as he said, in a very soft tone,

'You're fully aware that I want to end our engagement?'

'Yes, I'm fully aware of that,' she replied through whitened lips.

'And yet you insist on continuing with this farce?'

'I'm not giving you up,' she said stubbornly.

'You really believe you can force me to marry you?' He laughed harshly and Kathryn winced. 'You can think again, my girl!'

'I can't force you, of course not. But—but if our engagement's to be broken, then it'll be you who'll break it.'

'You'd have me marry you, knowing as I do that you deliberately trapped me into this engagement? That you took advantage of circumstances to bring about a situation which would so embarrass me that I'd have to offer you marriage?' His narrowèd eyes swept contemptuously over her. 'It has occurred to you, I suppose, that I can end this engagement—now?'

'Naturally it has; but there'll be considerable gossip—'

'Do you think I care about that?'

'You cared before,' she reminded him.

'I see. . . . So this is another ace you hold—or think you hold.' His fury died, but Kathryn saw an expression even more terrifying enter his eyes. 'Very well, Kathryn, we'll stay engaged—' He came close, to stand threateningly over her. 'Yes, we'll stay engaged—but you'll regret it. Believe me, you'll rue the day you ever kept me to my promise!' And with that he strode to the door and was gone.

Sinking into a chair, Kathryn put trembling hands to her temples. She felt utterly drained of energy. She had succeeded in preventing his immediate engagement to Delia, but had she really done any lasting good? He would never marry her, Kathryn—and she couldn't go on being engaged to him indefinitely. People were already expecting the wedding date to be announced and if it were delayed for any length of time there must inevitably be murmurings. And what of her parents? Impatiently ridding herself of that intrusion into her thoughts, she tried to concentrate on what had obviously been a threat on John's part. She would live to regret this day, he had vowed—and he meant it. What was he intending to do? But he couldn't inflict any real injury on her, she told herself; he had spoken in anger and bitterness, and as with her, words had been uttered which he probably did not mean.

Gradually her nerves settled, but her thoughts reverted to that night on the moors, when they had lain so close. And now this bitter angry scene, this disunion which must remain with them for ever, the icy contempt and hatred that John now felt for her—all these, after that intimacy, that sense of oneness that had come to them in the threat of a danger which they both knew could so easily have overtaken them. How strange, she thought, that whereas she herself had been profoundly affected by what happened on the moors, it had touched John not at all. He had felt no different about her after the adventure than before. Suddenly Kathryn's thoughts reverted to Michael, and what he had said about not being convinced that John would end the engagement. Kathryn frowned. Why should she think of that now? But even as she asked herself the question she saw again that hint of tenseness about John as he had stood by the fireplace a short while ago; momentarily it had softened him, dispelling the impression of hardness effected by the grimness of his features and the icy contempt in his eyes. *Had* John been going to inform her the engagement was at an end? In her eagerness to put in the first word she hadn't waited to see. Supposing he had been going to ask for an explanation? Kathryn's whole body began to tremble as she dwelt on this possibility. Why hadn't she waited? Sudden dejection flooded over her again. What was this wishful thinking? If John had desired an explanation he would have insisted on one despite her swift assertion that she had no intention of giving him up. Besides, his every word had conveyed the impression that he had wanted his freedom.

'You're fully aware that I want an end to our engagement?' he had said, and a moment later he had called it a farce.

No, Michael was very mistaken. John believed Delia and, in consequence, had no further desire to marry Kathryn.

They met again at dinner; John was frigidly silent throughout the meal. Coffee was brought to them in the sitting-room and immediately she had finished it Kathryn said she was going for a walk.

'You'll stay here with me.' The curt order took her by surprise. She had expected him to be relieved at the prospect of being left alone; he could not really want her with him, she knew, so what was his idea?

'I feel like some fresh air,' she began, rising from her chair.

'You've had plenty of fresh air today. Sit down.'

Kathryn's eyes flashed; his intention had not yet dawned upon her and she said defiantly,

'I'm going out, John, and you can't stop me.'

'Can't I?' His eyes were points of ice. 'You're engaged to me and you'll obey me. Should I wish to take a walk later, then you'll come with me—otherwise, we stay here until bedtime.'

His intention did then become perfectly clear.

'I see.' She looked at him steadily. 'Is this what you meant when you said I'd live to regret keeping you to your promise?'

'This is nothing, my dear Kathryn,' he returned on a half sneer. 'Obeying a small order like that's a mere trifle compared to what you will do.'

Kathryn sat back in her chair, but although she contrived to appear calm, she dwelt fearfully on that threat, trying to visualize what he had in mind. But again she told herself he could do her no real harm. Orders he might give, but if she made no move to defy him he would soon realize it was all ineffective and abandon the idea of revenge.

He read all the evening, while Kathryn just stared into the fire. But eventually she could tolerate it no longer and she rose from her chair.

' I'm going to bed, John,' she said firmly. ' Good night.'

He stood up, stifling a yawn.

' Yes, I'm tired too.' With a lightning move he took hold of her and before she could even guess at his intention she felt his mouth close upon hers. Struggling violently, she managed to turn her head away, but her face was instantly seized in a hurtful grip and jerked round again. This time she was helpless, and after admitting the futility of her struggles she desisted and stood there, passively enduring the brutal pressure of his lips. At last he released her ; she just stared up at him, her lovely eyes dark with pain and disbelief. And yet hadn't she concluded a while back that he could actually be cruel ? ' You're beautiful, I'll give you that,' he sneered. ' And most desirable.' He flicked his finger across her cheek. ' You don't appear to have enjoyed my kisses.' Kathryn's mouth moved convulsively, but no words came and John went on, still in the same sneering tones, ' You'll have to get used to them, I'm afraid—' He held her away from him and a hint of mockery entered his eyes. ' I'm within my rights in taking what I want . . . for we *are* engaged.'

' I understand, John,' she whispered and then, in a low but dignified voice, ' May I go now?'

Black anger touched his brow and Kathryn half expected him to strike her.

'Don't speak to me in that tone,' he warned softly, 'or I might retaliate in a way which would be even more undesirable than my kisses. Yes, you may go now.' Roughly he thrust her from him. 'Good night,' he said, and added in tones of sardonic humour, 'Sleep well, Kathryn—and pleasant dreams.'

CHAPTER IX

Just two more week-ends and then the house would be closed until the spring. Kathryn stood by the window in the Fitton bedroom, gazing out across the low hills to the two prominent features of Shutlinslow and the Cloud of Bosley. A spinning mist was coming down and a frown crossed her brow as a flash of memory took her back to that day on the moors, and the change in her life resulting from John's desire to see a little of the country around him. The change. . . . Never would she have believed she could endure treatment such as John was meting out to her. And yet her determination never wavered. Were she to give him up now he would instantly become engaged to Delia; Kathryn had never been so sure of anything in her life, because he and Delia were always together. And so she stuck stubbornly to her resolve, though the cost was high, and life at times became so unbearable that, up in her bedroom, she would resort to the relief of tears. Despising herself for this weakness, she would then half decide on some form of retaliation. But to defy John was only inviting trouble, and she had quite enough of that already. For her mother was asking when the wedding was to be; visitors were also inquiring about it. Michael was anxious because he had guessed what was happening, and even Andrea had put forth a tentative question, asking if anything were wrong.

'Wrong?' Kathryn had echoed lightly. 'In what way, Andrea?'

'Oh, nothing—really. You're pale these days and—and, Kathryn, forgive me for this, because I'm sure it sounds interfering, but the way John speaks to you at times—and in front of people—' She broke off and added, 'I'm terribly sorry, I shouldn't have said that. After all, it's nothing to do with me—or anyone else for that matter.'

Or anyone else. . . . Were people talking? But yes, they must be, for John never missed an opportunity of humiliating her, or giving her orders, in the presence of others. She knew this was a calculated plot designed to weaken her resolve. It had been going on for nearly a fortnight, and even though she did her utmost to avoid him, whenever they did come into contact Kathryn invariably suffered some indignity; but as none of this affected her feelings for her fiancé, her determination remained as strong as even.

She stiffened as she heard him in his bedroom, which was across from the Fitton Room. He knew she was in here, for she had mentioned her intention of changing the covers on the bed, and Kathryn waited for him to come in to her, steeling herself for any insult to which he might feel inclined to subject her.

She had not long to wait, and she turned as he entered, having to bend low to come through the doorway. His glance moved to the new cover, folded neatly on a chair by the bed, and then to Kathryn's slender figure, outlined against the window.

'Haven't you finished in here yet?' he inquired, not in the attractive drawl, but in a voice curt and clipped, the voice with which she had become so familiar in the beginning when he had been no more to her than the cool impersonal employer.

'I haven't started yet.'

'Then please do so at once. I have work for you to

do downstairs.'

'Work?' She threw him a questioning glance. 'It's almost lunch time, and this is my afternoon off.'

'It *was* your afternoon off. That's all finished.'

'Don't I get any time off, then?'

He came further into the room and stood looking down at her dispassionately.

'You talk as if you're still an employee of mine.'

'Aren't I?'

'You're my—fiancée, and that makes a slight difference.'

Moving over to the bed, Kathryn turned back the cover and began carefully to fold it.

'I'm still entitled to a little leisure time, John,' she told him seriously. 'My mother expects me this afternoon.'

'You're sure it's your mother you're going to see?' he asked crisply. 'It wasn't last Wednesday, was it?'

She glanced up, faint colour tinting her cheeks.

'Michael had a piece of netsuke which he thought might interest me. I did in fact buy it.'

'You collect netsuke?' he queried, subjecting her to a piercing scrutiny.

'I have a few pieces, yes.' Kathryn gave her attention to the cover again. Having folded it she placed it on the chair, taking off the new one and spreading it on the bed.

'You have some expensive hobbies,' he remarked on a faintly sneering note. 'Did Mr Southon help you with your netsuke collection?'

A trembling sigh escaped her. Having spread the cover, and straightened it to her liking, she stood up and faced him, her eyes unnaturally bright.

'Mr Southon didn't buy me anything at all. He gave me the presents that you know of, but I saved my salary and bought things like the netsuke—things which I like to own.' There was a hint of reproach in her voice and

157

for a brief moment she sensed an uncertainty about him, but it was gone instantly, replaced by the more familiar icy contempt.

'You're a clever and a scheming woman, Kathryn,' he said, his lip curling. 'But you're not quite clever enough. You'll never be mistress here, I can assure you of that, so the sooner you decide to return my ring the better it will be for us both.' Without giving her time to comment he turned and strode from the room. A moment later she heard his little radio, and the announcer's soft voice reading the news.

Immediately lunch was over Kathryn said she was going out.

'I must see my mother. She expects me to visit her once a week and, as you've said, I didn't visit her last week.'

'Very well, you may go; but be back here for dinner.'

Ignoring that order, which was calculated to bring some spirited retort, Kathryn said gently,

'Will it be all right if I take one of the cars?'

He opened his mouth to refuse; she waited breathlessly, for it was pouring with rain and the bus stop was over half a mile away.

'You can take the small one.'

'The very small one? But there's something wrong with the steering.'

'So you say. I didn't find anything wrong with it.' She shook her head.

'It is wrong, John. It went out of control on me.' His lip curled.

'Tell the truth. You're now too much of the lady to be seen driving the small car—'

'You know it isn't that! ' she cut in indignantly. ' I don't care which car I use—but I want it to be safe.'

'The small one's safe. Take that, or do without.'

She would use the bus, Kathryn decided, and went upstairs for her raincoat and umbrella. But no sooner had she stepped outside than the heavens opened, and she stepped back inside again. She couldn't walk half a mile in this. After waiting for about ten minutes she went in to fetch the car key. John was just coming downstairs and she turned to him.

'I'm going in the car—it isn't safe, John. . . .' He had reached the bottom of the stairs and, without even looking at her, he passed her and entered the Drawing Room. Shrugging resignedly, she went out to the garage and a few moments later she was gingerly trying out the car in the old drive. At the end of this was the Gate House, or the Dower House as it was originally. Reaching this, Kathryn pulled up sharply. Odd, but the steering seemed to be all right now. Turning the car round, she tried it again. Yes, John was right, there was nothing wrong with it . . . but there had been; she couldn't have made a mistake like that. The car was definitely out of control at one time when last she had it on the road, and she had mentioned it to John immediately on her return. He had said he would have it attended to, but he must have tested himself first, and found nothing wrong with it. No wonder he suspected her of not wanting to use it—but then he suspected her of all sorts of things these days, and Kathryn could not blame him, for he firmly believed her to be the clever scheming woman he had called her an hour or so ago. Always she tried to remember that; to remember he did not know the truth; for only in this way could she forgive him all the slights to which he subjected her.

She drove with extreme care, and very slowly, but by the time she arrived at her home she had begun to wonder if she had imagined a fault in the steering of the car, because it had given her no trouble at all. Perhaps on that other occasion she had not been fully concentrating on her driving. With most drivers there was the odd occasion when their mind would wander for a second, and their car would naturally swerve. Yes, it must have been her own fault, she concluded, feeling much happier now that she knew she could safely drive back to the Hall at a reasonable speed, for there was nothing quite so monotonous as having to go slowly when the road invited speed.

'You look pale, dear.' Her mother examined her face critically. 'It's the strain, I expect. Er—when is the wedding? Have you fixed the date yet?' Kathryn had not even taken her things off before the question came.

'Not yet, Mother.' She hung her coat in the hall and followed her mother into the spotless, cosy living-room. 'Are you all by yourself?'

'Your father's on two–ten this week—I told you on the phone.'

'Yes, I remember.' She sat down; the budgerigar flew out of his cage and settled on her shoulder. She put out a finger and he hopped on to it. 'Sammy . . . say hello.'

'Sammy . . . say hello.'

Smiling, Kathryn leant back in her chair. Behind the fine-meshed guard the fire was roaring in the grate—her mother loved huge fires. It was worse to be cold than hungry, she always maintained, and Kathryn had never really thought about it. For, in Britain anyway, there were few people these days who couldn't have both. Kathryn looked around. Her mother was a born home-maker, and the snug comfort found in her house was something which Kathryn had always appreciated. And eager as she was to fall in with Mr Southon's suggestion and live in at the Hall, she had for a while missed her home and her parents.

'I'll get the tea ready,' Mrs Ramsey said, after watching Kathryn with the bird. 'I've made some marmalade, and for all I say it myself it's really good.'

'I'll have some of that,' Kathryn returned eagerly. 'Have you made scones as well?'

Her mother nodded.

'We'll have a nicy cosy tea together, just the two of us.' A faint yearning in her voice made Kathryn look up, but Mrs Ramsey was already leaving the room, going into the bright little kitchen where she spent a great part of her life. Rising, Kathryn held her hand to the cage and the bird hopped inside. Then, taking a tablecloth from the drawer, she spread it on the table. Twenty minutes later she and her mother were seated by the fire, having their tea.

'I though you'd have fixed a date for the wedding.' Mrs Ramsey brought up the subject again, and Kathryn detected a note of anxiety in her voice as she added, 'You are happy about it, Kathryn? I mean, I'm thrilled at the idea of your marrying John, and being the lady of the manor, but I do want you to be happy too.'

'I'm happy—but we're not in love, Mother, and—and so it's—well, difficult sometimes.'

'You mean—? You can't mean that John's unkind, or anything? No, he'd never be; I knew he was a charming young man the moment you introduced us to him. And later, when we'd really had a long chat with him, both your father and I were thoroughly satisfied about your future. I said you'd both do very well, didn't I?'

'Yes, Mother,' she smiled, 'you did.'

'I expect you'll be fixing the wedding date soon,' went on Mrs Ramsey. 'Is it to be in the cathedral?'

Kathryn looked down at her plate. It was to have been in the ancient church, the church in which all the Fittons had worshipped, even though they had their own chapel inside the Hall. It was a most beautiful building of weathered sandstone and mellowed with age. The great yews in the churchyard were probably over a thousand years old, being entered in the Domesday Book nearly nine hundred years ago. Kathryn had been thrilled with the prospect of being married there, with the villagers out, laughing and throwing confetti. She had seen many village weddings since coming to Marbeck, and it was always like that. The villagers would gather outside the church, gossiping and waiting for the bride. It was an intimate affair, and sacred. Realizing her mother was expecting an answer, Kathryn said brightly,

'I—we'd rather be married at Marbeck church. I don't think John would like too big a wedding.' She wanted to change the subject, and she began talking about her sisters, who were supposed to be getting another flat.

'They're not looking,' her mother said with slight impatience. 'And it's so hard to keep the place tidy with them around. I'm always at it in here, and the bedrooms—well, I've no need to describe those to you!'

'No.' Kathryn laughed even while remembering that dreadful bedroom of Rita's. 'They don't get a scrap better, do they?'

'They don't grow up; though I must say they did try when they first came—when you made them leave the Hall, that was, but they've gradually drifted back into their old slipshod ways again.'

'There's nothing basically wrong with them, though,' Kathryn said staunchly. 'They're very young yet.'

'Rita's nineteen; she should be acquiring a little more sense by now.'

'I'll clear away and wash up,' Kathryn offered a little while later, when they had finished their tea. 'And then I must go, I suppose.'

'You suppose?' frowned Mrs Ramsey, looking sharply at her. 'What an odd thing to say, Kathryn.' A troubled pause and then, 'You are happy, child?'

'I've said so, Mother. But I've also reminded you that we're not in love.' *John* was not in love, she thought, an almost physical little ache in her heart. But at least he had liked her a little when they became engaged.

'No, dear, you've already said that, but—' She

162

broke off, her frown deepening. 'That girl who was at your party—the one John danced with several times—they weren't going about together, or anything like that?'

'They were very friendly,' Kathryn had to admit. 'Delia Slade, her name is. They live about three miles from the Hall.'

'They were friendly? You don't think . . . ? What am I saying?' she amended hastily. 'You and John are to be married, and what he once felt for another girl doesn't matter. He couldn't have felt anything really deep, otherwise he wouldn't have offered to marry you, would he?'

'No, Mother,' Kathryn agreed with a small sigh. Her mother was being far from tactful, but her words couldn't hurt; Kathryn was already just as much hurt as she could be. She felt nothing could make her more unhappy than she was at present.

'I'll see you next week, at the same time,' Kathryn said as she got into the car. 'Love to Dad, and Rita and Dawn.'

'I'll give it to them, dear. Goodbye—take care.'

'I will,' promised Kathryn, smiling. 'Don't stand at the door waving; it's too cold and wet.'

She was on a fairly quiet road when it happened. Having decided that there was no fault in the steering after all, Kathryn put her foot down on the accelerator and drove at her normal speed. She had just passed another car when, with a shock, she found the wheel useless in her hands; instinctively she jammed on the brakes. Some yards ahead, on the opposite side of the road, a lorry was parked; the driver was standing by his cab, doing something to the door. Utterly helpless to prevent it, Kathryn sat there while her car went careering across the road towards the man. She put her finger on the klaxon and kept it there. Was he deaf? she thought wildly. He looked up, gaped for a second and just as he jumped clear Kathryn closed her eyes tightly. . . .

Although greatly shocked, Kathryn had by some miracle escaped with cuts and bruises, although she remained unconscious for some time after being admitted to hospital.

John and her mother were at her bedside when she opened her eyes. She blinked uncomprehendingly from one to the other.

'She's coming round.' She heard his voice from a long way off—not the harsh contemptuous voice she had come to take for granted, but the soft and lazy drawl she loved.

'Thank God!' Her mother's anxious tones now; Kathryn smiled at her, then put a hand to her head. Bandages?

'What . . . ? Where . . . ?' She uttered a great sigh. 'I remember—' She sat up. 'That man! Is he—is he—'

'He jumped clear,' John reassured her quietly, and gently put her back on the pillow.

'Kathryn dear—oh, are you feeling all right? Are you sure there are no broken bones?' She asked the question of John; he shook his head.

'There are no broken bones, Mrs Ramsey.'

'How do you come to be here?' Kathryn asked. 'How did they find you?' She looked questioningly at John.

'The address was in your handbag. The police contacted me right away.'

'How long have I been here?'

'Only a few hours, dear,' her mother interposed, reaching down to clasp the hand lying on the bed cover. 'How are you feeling?' she asked again.

'Not too bad at all.' She paused and as memory flashed she could not suppress a shudder. 'I went into the lorry—but I wasn't going very fast by then,' she added, recalling that the *brakes* on the small car were certainly efficient.

'Don't think about it,' John said, and only then did everything return to Kathryn. She had told him about the steering. . . . Her eyes fluttered to his; she saw remorse there, and—concern? Yes, deep concern. That didn't mean a thing, of course. He would be concerned no matter who it had been, and he would also feel guilty. No, that expression had no particular significance. His opinion of her could not undergo a change simply because of this accident.

'The nurse is here,' Mrs Ramsey looked across the ward. 'I think we'll have to go.' She glanced at her watch. 'The buses run every half hour, so I'll not have long to wait.'

'I'll take you,' offered John, turning as the nurse reached the bed. 'She'll be able to come home tomorrow, you said?'

'That's what the doctor thinks. She'll have to be kept in bed for a few days, of course, but it's the shock more than any actual injury.'

'I'll see she stays in bed, naturally.' Again that lazy, attractive drawl, but Kathryn frowned. John had said scarcely anything to her, had not even asked how she was feeling. Her mother had, though, so perhaps he considered it superfluous to ask the same question— which of course it was. And yet it seemed to Kathryn that he didn't want her at the Hall, and in any case she ought to be with her own family. She asked her mother if she could go home.

'I'd be better there,' she added. Conscious of John's having given a little start, Kathryn turned her head to look at him. Was it imagination, or was there a trace of hurt in **his** attitude at her request to be taken to her own home?

'Certainly you can, dear. The girls—they're still as rowdy as ever, but they'll just have to do without their transistors and record players for a while,' she added decisively.

The nurse left them, obviously giving them the opportunity of discussing these arrangements.

'Kathryn will need quietness, Mrs Ramsey,' said John in soft yet inexorable tones. 'I think she'll be better in her own room at the Hall.'

'Yes . . . well. . . .' Mrs Ramsey's voice tailed off uncertainly. It was clear she was not intending to argue with the man whom she expected would soon be her son-in-law. 'The girls are noisy, as I said.' She looked down at her daughter. 'John's right, dear. Much as I'd love to have you at home, and take care of you myself, I do think you'll be much more comfortable at the Hall.'

Kathryn's eyes were again drawn to her fiancé's face. Did he genuinely want her—or was his conscience troubling him? This latter was the case, she knew, but she made no further request to be taken to her parents' home and it was arranged that John should come for her after lunch on the following day.

She sat in the back of the car, cosily wrapped in rugs. Her head was bandaged and so were her arms, but apart from some superficial scratches on her face and legs, she had no further injuries. Immediately on entering the house she went up to her room. A fire had been lighted, more for cosiness than for the heat it gave, for central heating had been installed throughout the house in Mr Southon's day. Kathryn had been in bed a mere five minutes when John came up. He stood there looking down at her, so tall and straight, his handsome face clouded, his mouth taut, and yet in no way grim or harsh.

'I'm sorry, Kathryn,' he said, and she sensed an awkwardness that was completely out of character. It would be difficult for him to voice his regret, she decided understandingly, seeing there was no basic change in his opinion of her. 'I should have listened to you. I had tried the car out, when you told me of the fault, and it seemed to be perfectly all right. I'm sorry,' he repeated. 'This is all my fault.'

But Kathryn shook her head and told him gently,

'No, John, it isn't your fault at all. The car did appear to be all right—I even decided I'd imagined it, because the steering behaved perfectly on my way there. It was on my way back that it happened, as you know.'

'Nevertheless, you'd suspected a fault and I should have listened to you. One can't afford to have a faulty car on the road.'

During the next day or two Kathryn had the impression that although John still detested her, still believed all he had heard, he also had some other feeling for her . . . a feeling of which he was ashamed. This persisted, being revealed in the way he spoke to her and the way he looked. He was so gentle, and at times even tender. Kathryn would bask in these moods, yet each time she would be jerked back to reality by a sudden harsh word or icy glance of contempt. It was as if John were fighting something; but the more Kathryn thought about it the more impatient she became with herself. The bump on her head must have affected her in some peculiar way, she at last decided, and resolved not to allow John's changing moods to tease her any longer.

On the Sunday he came up to her, bringing Mrs Percival and another of the old ladies whom Kathryn had befriended.

'Two visitors for you,' he smiled. 'Two very concerned visitors, I may add.' He fetched chairs for them and placed them by the bed.

'Miss Ramsey, dear, are you feeling better?' Mrs Percival's vivid blue eyes gazed anxiously down at her. 'What a blessing it was no worse.'

'I'm feeling fine, as a matter of fact,' Kathryn said, smiling. 'I'm only lying down because I've just had a doze. Normally I sit up and read. I feel so well that I know I should be up and working.' John looked at her strangely. Did he consider her to be merely saying this for effect? Was he mentally calling her a hypocrite?

'Nonsense, dear. You must rest; you've had a nasty jolt. We read about it in the paper, and were so dreadfully anxious. I wanted to come at once, but what with my heart, and my arthritis—well, buses are no good to me, and in any case I can't walk even to the bus stop.' She looked up at John and smiled charmingly at him. She must have been very beautiful when she was young, Kathryn thought, for she was lovely now, with a fresh complexion and scarcely any wrinkles. 'I rang the Hall and your nice kind fiancé offered to bring me. Ellen wanted to come too, and so here we are.'

John had offered to fetch her friends. . . . His face was set, as if he resented being referred to as a nice kind man. He hadn't been kind . . . was that why he resented it?

'I'll take you back when you're ready,' he offered. 'Kathryn will ring the bell if you want tea. I must go now—' He shook his head wonderingly. 'We have more visitors than ever today. I'd have thought they'd have dwindled to a mere handful by now.'

'Always for these last two week-ends we have this spurt,' Kathryn explained. 'It must be because we're going to be closed for a long while. The people want to have a last look, as it were.'

'I see; that explains it. We're to expect another big crowd next week-end, then?'

'Bigger than this, I should say—if the weather's fine, that is.'

Kathryn had another visitor later that day, a visitor she could very well have done without. But Delia's expression was one of deep concern as, entering the room in front of John, she stepped over to the bed.

'Those awful bandages, they're so large! Are you

much hurt, Kathryn?' The voice, so soft and anxious. Kathryn felt quite sick, wishing already that she had refused to see Delia when, with some hesitation, John had come up and informed her that both Delia and her parents were here, and they would all like to see her.

'I know how you must feel about Delia,' he had said curtly. 'But please remember she was rambling, and didn't know what she was saying.'

Kathryn had stared at him then, for while he was talking he all the time avoided her eyes, and his comment about Delia not knowing what she was saying was undoubtedly spoken in the most peculiar way. But his gaze was expressionless and Kathryn began to wonder if her imagination were playing her tricks again.

'I'll see her,' Kathryn agreed, adding, 'Mr and Mrs Slade?—they're coming up too, you say?'

'In a short while. They're deep in conversation with some of the visitors whom they know, having met them on holiday, I believe they said.'

After showing Delia into the room John went downstairs again, leaving them together.

'No, Delia, I'm not much hurt. But John must have already told you?'

Ignoring that, Delia sat down on the chair Mrs Percival had recently vacated. She crossed her legs and leant back comfortably. Her eyes were half closed yet searching; Kathryn put on a bright smile for her benefit and the narrowed gaze became almost baleful.

'You've been very lucky.' The sneer was barely discernible, but it was there all the same. 'John seems quite concerned about you. He maintains the accident was his fault, although he won't say why.' It was a question, but Kathryn ignored it, her interest being with Delia's first sentence. She said without any effort at tact,

'You say I'm lucky. Do you mean I'm lucky because my injuries are light . . . or because John's concerned about me?'

'The gloves are off, eh?'

'They've been off for some time, Delia,' came the quiet rejoinder. Kathryn was sitting propped up in bed —a dainty jacket draped round her shoulders. Her hair was attractively spread, a gleaming golden mass against the whiteness of the pillows. 'But I never dreamed for one moment you'd go to those great lengths to injure me,' she added, fixing Delia's gaze squarely. 'It was despicable!'

'Nothing of the kind. I did John a good turn. He knows now what you are.' Delia brought out a cigarette case and opened it. Without asking permission she lit a cigarette and inhaled deeply, blowing the smoke straight up into the air and watching it for a while. 'I expected you to give him up,' she added, her gaze returning to Kathryn.

'I've no intention of giving him up.'

'He doesn't want you—you must be aware of that?'

Had they been talking about her? Undoubtedly, otherwise Delia wouldn't know that John didn't want her.

'I intend to stay engaged to him—'

'He wants his freedom!' All restraint dropped from Delia; she was like a savage almost, her nostrils flaring and her eyes burning with anger and frustration. 'I expected him to throw you over—'

'Yes, you did, but your hateful plan misfired there, didn't it?'

'I forgot to reckon on his sense of honour. He'd consider himself held by his promise.'

That was not so; John did not consider himself held. He remained engaged to her only because he wanted to avoid unsavoury talk. But he was only waiting—waiting for the day when Kathryn, unable to tolerate his treatment any longer, would herself break off their engagement. However, Kathryn naturally did not feel inclined to divulge this slip to Delia, so she merely agreed —not verbally, but with a shrug of her shoulders. The action infuriated Delia and her anger flared again.

' How long do you think you can hold him, despite this idea he has of honour? You've schemed and plotted in order to be mistress here, but you'll never be that! John will never stoop to marrying a girl like you, so the sooner you return his ring the better!'

The colour drained from Kathryn's cheeks. Those words . . . almost exactly the words John had spoken to her. It could be coincidence, she supposed, but . . . no, she felt sure they had been talking together. And if they had, they must be on very intimate terms. John, it seemed, did want to marry Delia. For one fleeting moment Kathryn was tempted to say she would release him, to tell Delia she could have him— But her half-hearted decision was thrust away; she would stick to her resolution no matter what the cost. Completely deceived by Delia, John thought marriage to her was what he wanted, that in it lay the promise of perfect happiness. ' Well, I know better,' Kathryn said to herself, her eyes glinting with determination. ' I won't let him ruin his life, no matter how he might hate me for it!'

John came up later, and, looking down at the lovely figure Kathryn made, sitting there against the snowy pillows, a most odd expression entered his eyes. He seemed baffled and uncertain, but mingling with this was a softness which was by no means lost on Delia. Her eyes narrowed almost to slits, and she had difficulty in maintaining the charming feminine manner which was invariably kept for John—or any other man friend in whose company she happened to be.

' How is our invalid now?' John asked, sitting down on the bed. He had not glanced at Delia, but he did turn as, leaving Kathryn no time to answer his question, she said with forced lightness,

' Kathryn's obviously feeling quite well, John, because

her conversation's most spirited.'

'Indeed?' John's brows lifted inquiringly, but he gave no smile in return for the dazzling one Delia flashed at him. 'I hope you haven't exhausted yourself, Kathryn?'

So he had guessed they'd been sparring? Did he care that she might have exhausted herself?

'I think I remained quite calm, John, thank you,' she returned smoothly, and an appreciative curve of his lips told her he understood what she was thinking.

'Mr and Mrs Slade will be here directly,' he said, 'and that is all for today. It's rest from now on.'

'But you said I could get up for dinner,' she reminded him impulsively, forgetting Delia's presence altogether. 'Please may I?' Her tones were childishly sweet and clear; John's voice was gentle as he said,

'If I made a promise then I must keep to it.'

'You know you promised.'

'Yes, I know I did, and, as I've said, I must keep to it. You shall get up for dinner.'

'Have we anyone coming?' she inquired on a little wistful note. In addition to the Slades, one or two other newly-made friends of John's had been coming to dinner, and Bernard and Andrea had also dined with them on a couple of occasions.

John shook his head.

'We've no one coming this evening.' He was smiling at her and she suddenly felt happy.

If this softened attitude would only remain . . . if John would treat her with just a little more friendliness, then perhaps an occasion would arise where she could explain, tell him her side of the story. Hope brought a lightness to her heart; it was revealed in her expression, but, catching Delia's eyes, Kathryn felt her pulses race. Why this sudden fear? It was ridiculous, she told herself impatiently. Delia had done her worst and there was nothing more she could do, absolutely nothing.

CHAPTER X

The dinner was a pleasant meal, with John chatting to Kathryn all the time and, for a little while at least, seeming to forget what he had learned from Delia.

'Next Sunday will be the last until the spring,' he was saying as Emily came in to serve the second course. 'I'll be glad, Kathryn. I'm going to enjoy having the place to myself.' He stopped, as if aware of the significance of his words, but although he smiled he made no attempt to alter the meaning of those words. 'We must expect a very large crowd, you said?'

'If the weather is fine, yes.' She gave a little grimace. 'Everybody buys guide books and plans of the house, so we have more work than usual with the accounts, for the takings will be extra high.'

'I suppose we'll cope with the books, but what about the crowds? We're two students short.'

She hesitated.

'Michael might like to come in,' she suggested, watching his face closely.

His eyes flickered, but he agreed that it would be advantageous to have a man in with the great knowledge possessed by Michael.

'I'll give him a ring,' he ended decisively. 'Let's hope he'll accept.'

'I feel sure he will. He loves this place.'

'So I've noticed.'

'So many people do.' She helped herself to condiments and then, with faint anxiety, 'Are you intending to re-open the Hall in the spring?'

'I haven't decided. Have you never considered how pleasant it would be to have this place to yourself?' The question startled her and she glanced up swiftly. Then, flushing with embarrassment, she lowered her head. His question was clearly not directed at her personally; he was merely asking for her opinion.

' It would be nice, I admit. But so many people come now; it seems a shame not to open it.'

' For the money, you mean?' he queried, watching her closely.

' No, not merely for the money. So much pleasure is given to those people. Almost without exception they're lovers of beautiful things and, as you must have noticed, they treat everything with great care and respect. In all the six years we've been open we haven't had a thing either broken or stolen.'

' That's a wonderful record, wonderful.' A thoughtful pause and then, ' Perhaps I shall open it— yes, I mustn't deprive these people of the pleasure they get from coming to my home.'

' I'm glad. We'll—you'll have nearly six months of privacy, for you don't open till Easter.' If he noticed her hesitation and amendment he chose to ignore them, and they chatted on in the same vein until the meal was finished. Later, after they had been sitting reading for some time, John glanced at the clock and told Kathryn it was time she went back to bed.

' Oh, but. . . .' The evening had been so pleasant, so promising, that she was actually fearful of ending it. ' I'm not a bit tired.'

' Nevertheless you must go back to bed,' he said firmly. ' It's only four days since the accident; you've done very well indeed and we want you to continue doing so.'

Resignedly she rose, shutting up her book and laying it on the chair.

' I think I'll take it with me,' she said, picking it up again.

' Can't you sleep?' He sounded anxious, she thought, as he waited for her reply.

' I sleep very well—but it's early.' Faint apology in those last words and his eyes flickered with amusement.

' Obviously you don't like being sent to bed early.'

His words amazed her. Was he really teasing her? Dared she broach the subject of what Delia had to.d him? Was this a propitious occasion for relating her version of the story and leaving him to decide whether or not he still preferred to believe Delia? No, perhaps it was not the right time, she decided, reluctant to risk spoiling the happiest evening she had spent since the night of her birthday party. Given a little longer, John might be more approachable. Another week, perhaps. . . .

By the following Sunday Kathryn was well enough to take up her usual duties and although John at first raised some objection, she did finally persuade him. for even by half-past ten in the morning the crowds were streaming through the gates. It was a beautiful sunny day, with a clear sky and scarcely a breath of wind; just the sort of day to bring families out for a run in the country.

' Take things easy, then,' John advised in the some-what peremptory tones he had recently begun to use to her. ' At the least sign of tiredness you're to go into the sitting-room and rest.'

' I will,' she promised, thrilled and strangely excited by his concern, and by his tone of voice. ' But I don't think I'll feel in the least tired.'

There was no doubt about the change in him since the accident. Yet always Kathryn was conscious of that underlying sense of self-contempt within him. And although on the whole this past week had been one of quiet harmony, there were still occasions when John would snap at her, and even deliberately subject her to some form of humiliation, and Kathryn gained the impression that any kindness shown to her was eventually regretted.

If this were true, then it meant that although he believed what he had heard, he could not hate Kathryn as he felt he should. With this conviction growing steadily as the days passed, Kathryn decided that, at the first suitable opportunity, she would talk to John, explaining the circumstances in which she had said those things Delia had so cleverly twisted, and denying ever having thought of exploiting the mishap that had occurred up on the moors. He could then judge for himself—and somehow Kathryn felt convinced he would no longer condemn her.

By the middle of the afternoon the house was packed, and Kathryn was in fact beginning to feel a little jaded. However, she had no intention of giving in, for although Michael was here, looking after the first floor, they were still a man short.

'They'll begin drifting out soon,' she told John, glancing at her watch. It was after four and the sun was already low in the sky.

'Are you tired?'

'Not very.' And, seeing his expression she added hastily, 'I'll be all right, truly.'

Michael called her from over the banister rail and she left John and went to him.

'These priest holes,' Michael said when she reached him. 'Are these kids allowed to play in them?'

Kathryn had to laugh. It was not the first time children had played an exciting game of hide and seek, using the priest holes.

'Bring them out, Michael—but be cautious; their doting mums are around, don't forget.'

He grinned and raised his two thumbs.

'I'll watch myself,' he promised, grinning, and then, softly in her ear, 'You look happy. Did the car accident put things right between you two?'

'It hasn't worked a miracle, if that's what you mean.'

'Delia? Are they still as thick as ever?'

'They're still friendly.'

'Hmm. . . . But John's fond of the parents, isn't he?'

She nodded.

'Yes, and so am I.'

'They're nice. How did they come to produce poison like Delia?' And without giving her time to reply he went on to ask what Delia was doing here today.

'She's here? I haven't seen her.'

Michael pointed to the window.

'Her car's down there on the front. I didn't see her arrive, but the car's been there for at least half an hour. What's she doing here?' he asked again.

'I expect she's come to see John—what other reason could there be? As you know, neighbours often pop in on open days for a chat with John.'

'Well, watch her. As I've said, she's poison.'

Not attaching much importance to Michael's words, Kathryn returned to her duties downstairs. People were leaving—for the doors were to be closed at five o'clock— and for the first time Kathryn was glad to see them go. She felt thoroughly tired and all she wanted was to sit down and rest. Where was Delia? she wondered. But as neither she nor John were anywhere about Kathryn surmised that they were in the sitting-room having tea.

By a quarter to five the house was almost empty, but as always a few stragglers remained. A little group were in the Compass Room when Kathryn went up to take a look round. They were admiring the four-poster bed and as she entered one of them passed some remark. It was plain they were seeking for information, and although she wasn't feeling at all up to it Kathryn obligingly told them something of its history.

'It came from Lymphe Castle,' she said. 'But at some period it has been in the Boswell family, for here you have the Boswell arms.'

'Not the family of Boswell the diarist?'

'The same. Johnson's biographer could have slept on this bed; he probably did.' Kathryn stayed in the room and presently the small group of people drifted out, leaving her alone. But almost at once Delia entered; she must have been listening, for she said with undisguised sarcasm,

'How clever you are, Kathryn. You know everything about this house, don't you? And the history of every stick of furniture?'

'It's my job to know these things.' Her voice was a little husky, revealing her tiredness, and Delia's eyes glinted with satisfaction.

'John's making you work, and very sensible of him!'

'Why have you come up here?' Kathryn asked, moving across the room with the intention of closing the window. 'If you want John he's in the Chapel—or was, a moment ago.'

'I came to speak to you.'

'Oh?' Kathryn turned inquiringly.

'How long are you going to persist in this stubborn attitude?' she rasped. 'John's going to hate you more and more as time goes on, so it's not as if it's going to do you a bit of good.'

'I'm not discussing my fiancé with you,' returned Kathryn quietly. She closed the window and then moved to the door, standing there waiting for Delia to leave. When Delia made no attempt to do so Kathryn went on to say she was closing the room and locking the door. 'I don't want anyone in here at this time; it's almost five and I want everyone out of the house by then.'

'Fiancé!' Delia's eyes blazed. 'And *you* don't want anyone coming in here! *You* want everyone out by five— Who do you think you are?—the mistress here already! I suppose John's changed attitude's given you confidence. You think you've got him where you want him, but we'll see.' Her face was a mask of hate and frustration as she added, 'You'll never be mistress here, Kathryn Ramsey, never—so you might just as well get out now!'

Kathryn's face was white; never had she imagined anyone could so lose control as to talk and act in this disgusting way. It was unthinkable that John should become bound to such a woman, and this outburst only served to strengthen her resolution to save John from the disaster into which his own folly, and his ignorance of Delia's character, could lead him.

'I'm engaged to John,' she said with quiet dignity, 'and, as I've already told you, I'm staying engaged to him. And now, if you'll allow me to close the door . . . ?' Her tones and manner added fuel to the fire of Delia's wrath and, with a vicious swing, she turned and made for the door. Behind her an exquisite little pot-pourri jar which had stood on the table by the bed lay on the floor, smashed to fragments. Delia stopped and looked around.

'How careless you are, Kathryn,' she exclaimed before Kathryn could even open her mouth to speak. 'John was telling me the jar was very valuable. He's not going to be pleased about the breakage, is he?'

'Delia, how could you! This was so beautiful—'

'Me?' Delia lifted her eyebrows in mock surprise. 'I've just remarked on *your* carelessness.'

'I understand.' Kathryn spoke to herself, for Delia had gone. Stooping, she began to pick up the pieces. John had liked this jar, and even decided to take it into one of the private rooms where he could enjoy its beauty. Delia was right, he wasn't going to be pleased. And it was evident that she, Kathryn, would bear the brunt of his anger, for Delia would never admit to breaking it.

The pieces were scattered everywhere, and Kathryn searched carefully, hoping she had found every one. Then she went to her room and fetched her own little jar. She had bought it some time ago, believing it to be exactly the same as the one in Mr Southon's possession. They would make a pair, she thought, but on getting it home, she discovered one or two slight differences. They were hardly discernible, but Kathryn changed her mind about putting it in the Compass Room with the other.

Placing it on the bedside table, Kathryn stepped back, eyeing it critically. It was almost identical and she could only hope that John had not examined the other so minutely that he would detect the substitution.

The first real frosts came as a shock, putting the abrupt
end to the Indian summer. Every golden leaf was
stripped from the trees, and the fields and hedges were
thickly coated with rime. But in the sitting-room all was
cosy, with shaded wall lights adding to the glow from a
fire of blazing pine logs.

Kathryn sat alone, one of the account books open on
her lap and several others on the floor beside her. For
some reason there was a difference of quite a large sum of
money between the takings at the turnstile and the actual
amount Kathryn had given to John. He himself had
done the books, but had now passed them to Kathryn for
checking. She had sat down feeling confident of discovering the mistake and anticipating a word of praise
from John. But to her surprise she had not found the
mistake, and now it appeared that the sum of money was
missing. The implications of this did not at first strike
her, but when it did she found herself trembling and
going through the books once more, with almost frantic
haste. The result was the same, and she stared at John
anxiously when, just before lunch time he came in to her
and glanced down inquiringly.

' It's a mystery,' she admitted. ' I can't imagine
what's happened.' She paused and added reluctantly,
' It can't be due to mistakes in the change; the sum's far
too large.'

He looked thoughtfully at the books on the floor.

' I hadn't much hope of your finding it. I'd already
gone over the figures several times.'

She could very well imagine his doing so, and she now
wondered at her initial confidence in discovering a mistake. It seemed to Kathryn that he looked curiously at
her and a tremor of actual fear entered her voice as she
said,

' We must find it. It can't just have disappeared.'

'That's exactly what it seems to have done.' The drawl was there, but his voice was also sharp and curt and, to Kathryn's imagination, it carried a hint of accusation.

She felt helpless and could only say, in deeply distressed tones, that with the handling of such large sums of money invariably there must be times when discrepancies occurred.

'You've been short before?' This time there was no mistaking the sharpness of his tone. His eyes bored into her; Kathryn could not hold his gaze and she inclined her head, miserably aware that this could very well be taken as an indication of guilt on her part. She was almost ready to cry. For this to happen, just when she had decided to talk to him, to try and convince him of her innocence.

'We have been short,' she owned. 'But the amounts were very small.'

A pause followed; John seemed to be trying to read her thoughts and this only served to make her feel more flustered—and guilty.

'Well,' he sighed at last, 'I'm afraid we shall have to write it off, Kathryn, for despite what you say it has in fact disappeared.'

'But we can't leave it,' she cried. 'That would be unsatisfactory for us both!'

'Can you remember having left the money—if only for a moment—before handing it to me?'

She shook her head.

'No, I didn't leave it,' she replied miserably. 'That is—' She had left the money, she recollected. But only for a moment or two, while she went upstairs to close a window. The last of the visitors had gone, though, and in any case Delia was there all the time, so no one could have tampered with it.

'Yes? You remember something?'

'No—well, that is, I did leave it for a short while, on

the table in the hall, but Delia was there, otherwise I wouldn't have left it. And there were no visitors in the house.'

He frowned in thought.

'You're sure all the visitors had gone?'

'Quite sure; I'd locked the front door. Besides,' she reminded him, 'no one could have touched it while Delia was there.'

'No. . . .' His eyes kindled strangely. 'What makes you so sure she was there all the time?'

'She was looking at the old map on the wall; I only went up to the first landing to close a window, and she was still looking at it when I came down.'

'I see.' Again that odd kindling of his eyes. Kathryn wished with all her heart that she could read his thoughts. Was he blaming her?—silently accusing her of theft? 'Well, as you say, it's a mystery, and all we can do is forget it.' Stooping, he picked up the books lying on the floor, then he held out his hand for the one she had on her knee. She gave it to him, her eyes dark and unhappy. His expressionless gaze met hers for a long moment and then without another word he left the room, closing the door softly behind him. There seemed such cold finality about the click of the latch; it was as if that very sound conveyed to Kathryn the hopelessness of the task she had set herself.

And as she sat there staring unseeingly into the fire, she gradually accepted defeat, for this mysterious disappearance of the money had taken every bit of fight out of her. It was enough to combat the wicked machinations of Delia, but to have fate against her too. . . . A frown suddenly crossed Kathryn's brow. It was too much of a coincidence. . . . Delia was in the hall, alone. . . .

'I mustn't think such things,' she whispered, beginning to tremble. 'No, I must not. . . .'

The following day her parents paid an unexpected visit. They had been into Macclesfield and had decided to come along and see her and John. Although glad to see them, Kathryn felt some dismay at the idea of the four of them sitting there conversing, with her parents in sublime ignorance of the real situation. However, there was nothing to be done about it and she smilingly let them in, closing the door behind them.

'If it's not convenient we won't stay,' her father began, glancing towards the stairs. John was just coming down and, turning, Kathryn drew a deep breath. How handsome he was! And the way he carried himself; once again she likened him to the aristocratic Fittons. He caught her glance, and the most odd expression entered his eyes. 'We don't want to inconvenience you, John. Don't hesitate to say if we've come at an awkward time.'

'Kathryn's parents are always welcome,' he told him graciously, holding his hand out to take Mrs Ramsey's coat. 'After all, we are soon to be related.' Kathryn's eyes flew to his. He was looking at her with a most odd expression, and his mouth had curved into a tender line. What could have happened? she asker herself breathlessly.

John led them into the sitting-room and told Kathryn to order tea. She went into the kitchen herself to help and when she came back with the tray she was utterly dismayed to hear her mother saying,

'When is the wedding to be, John? Will it be before the end of the year?'

'It's for Kathryn to say, but I'm sure it will be before the end of the year—' Rising swiftly, he took the tray from Kathryn's trembling hands. 'What's the matter, child? I thought you were going to drop it.'

And you were right, she said, but to herself. Something *had* happened, but her mind was in such chaos she couldn't even begin to fathom what it was. As the afternoon wore on her curiosity increased until it could scarcely be contained, and it was actually a relief when at last she and John stood at the door watching the car disappearing round the curve of the drive.

No sooner had John closed the door than she turned to him. ' John, what is it?'

' What's what, my dear?' Taking her hand, he led her into the Drawing Room, where a fire glowed brightly in the grate. ' What made you change your mind about leaving me?' he asked without preamble, and Kathryn stared at him in blank astonishment.

' How do you know I intended leaving you?'

' That day—when I'd looked round for a while and couldn't find you I went up to your room; you had obviously been packing—or attempting to pack,' he amended with some amusement.

' The door was locked,' she began.

' I've a master key, you know that.'

' I forgot.' She felt the gentle movement of his fingers on the back of her hand and she looked up at him again, bewilderment in her eyes.

' Why didn't you say something then—when I came in, I mean?

' That was my intention, because there was so much I didn't understand. That exhibition of Delia's, for example, any fool could see it had been rehearsed—'

' You knew!'

' I knew the whole scene was put on so that I could be acquainted with certain things you'd said, and also hear about your nefarious scheme for—er—trapping me into marriage.'

' You didn't believe her?' Kathryn shook her head dazedly. ' But you *did* believe her, John. You must have because of the way you treated—I mean—oh, you must have!'

' I admit I was stunned at the time—and more so because you made no effort to defend yourself. That was why I cleared off the following day. I wanted to think. However, as I knew the " rambling " was a sham, I concluded that Delia had probably lied into the bargain. Your acceptance of the situation still puzzled me, but by this time I had an open mind—I neither believed Delia nor disbelieved her. You were the one who could explain, and I came back here to talk to you.'

'To talk?' So those suspicions she had so swiftly dismissed were correct. He had been going to ask for an explanation. 'Why did I act so impulsively?' she cried. 'If only I'd let you speak first!'

'It would have saved all the misunderstandings. You see, the discovery that you'd intended leaving me strengthened my belief in you. I was convinced of your innocence, convinced that even had you said any of those things attributed to you, they had been exaggerated, twisted by Delia.' He stopped and suddenly the softness went from his eyes and he glowered down at her. 'Then you came in and confounded me by giving me to understand that you had in fact taken advantage of that situation up on the moors. So I had to believe Delia, even though I still knew she'd staged the whole scene. Obviously then I wanted my freedom, but you stood there, defiant, and blatantly informing me that you'd never give me up, and there wasn't a thing I could do about it. You as good as said I'd have to marry you—marry you? I could have killed you!'

Kathryn put a trembling hand to her cheek. Although dazed by all he said, she could hear one sentence ringing out clearly above all the rest. 'I could have killed you!'

'John,' she faltered, looking up at him wonderingly, 'do you l-love me?'

'Love you—!' He still glowered at her—and his kisses were far from gentle. 'Does that tell you whether I love you or not?'

'Yes—yes, it d-does,' she managed, thoroughly shaken. Gradually his arms relaxed and she was in a gentle embrace, her head against his breast. 'What happened?' she asked at length. 'Something happened today . . . ?' She felt his lips caressing her hair and he did not answer her immediately.

'Were you so afraid of me that you couldn't tell me you'd broken the pot-pourri jar?' he queried with faint reproach.

She tilted her head to look at him.

'You know?'

'I saw a piece of it on the floor. I was completely baffled, because the complete jar was there on the table. But on examining it I knew it wasn't the original. Then I recalled having seen a similar jar in your room.' Releasing her, he drew a small note from his pocket. 'This was what you intended leaving, I presume?' He unfolded it to let her see.

'You—? She blinked. 'Where did you get that?'

'It was in the pot-pourri jar. Why were you afraid of telling me?' he asked again and, when she remained silent, 'Did you break it?'

She shook her head.

'No . . . no, I didn't.'

'Then who— One of the visitors?' He shook his head. 'It couldn't have been, because in that case you'd have told me. You're shielding someone. . . . There are only two people whom you would shield, Michael and Delia. But if Michael had broken that jar he'd immediately have owned up. So Delia broke it?' She merely nodded and he went on gravely, 'Do you realize if Dedia hadn't broken that jar I'd never have found this note?'

'You wouldn't, no. But—but I can't really see what difference the note makes, John.'

He held it out, pointing to one line.

' "Were our engagement based on something stronger than necessity, perhaps I could explain. . . .".' He smiled tenderly at her. 'What were you really saying, my love? Tell me.'

She hesitated shyly.

'I was really saying that, if you cared, then I could
186

easily have explained.'

'If I cared . . . and you were, by those words, telling me that you cared, that you loved me.' He took her in his arms again and kissed her tenderly on the lips. 'When did you know, my darling?'

'I think it had been coming on for some time—'

'Coming on?' he ejaculated. 'You sound as if it were some sort of disease!'

She laughed, but after a little while she confessed that she had known for sure when she had lain beside him, so close, up on the moors.

John heaved a great sigh.

'It wouldn't have done for us to have been marooned up there too long,' he admitted. 'I shall never know how I resisted taking you in my arms.'

'But you did,' she reminded him solemnly.

'In a purely platonic manner, though. But I loved you, Kathryn.'

'No—' She shook her head. 'You couldn't have, not then.'

'Why not?' He was puzzled, and she went on to remind him that he had mentioned their marriage would not be based on love. 'I did say that,' he admitted, 'but I really meant it wouldn't be based on mutual love.' And he added, teasingly, 'You see, darling, how was I to know that with you it had " been coming on for some time"?' Kathryn's grey eyes brimmed with laughter, but she said nothing, merely lifting her face, inviting his kiss. 'You haven't answered my question,' he reminded her, some time later. 'What made you change your mind about leaving me?'

'I'd been to see Michael.'

'So you said,' came the crisp response, and Kathryn's eyelids fluttered. Surely he wasn't jealous of Michael!

'He advised me to stay—'

'You discussed me with Michael!'

'Oh . . . just listen a moment—'

'I'm listening!'

After a rather frightened hesitation Kathryn explained, as tactfully as she could, and to her relief John's little spurt of anger died.

'You were saving me from myself? You honestly believed I could be taken in by anyone like Delia Slade?'

'You did seem to like her,' Kathryn reminded him, half apologetically.

'At first, yes, I must admit I did.'

'And after my birthday party, when you heard those awful things, you were with her a great deal then.'

'Because I wanted to hurt you—make you believe I didn't care a rap for you.'

'It's been all my fault, hasn't it?' she said contritely. 'I thought I was doing it for the best. I couldn't bear to think of your being married to anyone like—like Delia.'

There was silence in the room for a while and then John said softly,

'Kathryn darling, I don't want you to worry your lovely head about that money. Promise me you won't, dearest?'

'But, John—'

'I know what happened to it. . . .' A small pause and then, 'And I rather think you do too.' She made no answer and he added, 'Did Delia tell you I'd been commenting on your accepting gifts from Mr Southon?' Kathryn hesitated and he added, 'You believed her?'

'At first,' she owned apologetically. 'But not afterwards.' The catch in her voice revealed a little of what she had suffered; John kissed her again, then led her over to the fire. Sinking into the great armchair, he pulled her gently on to his knee. Twilight had fallen as they talked, and the glowing coals showered the room with a deep crimson radiance. Kathryn nestled her head against John's shoulder and a smile of sweet contentment touched her lips.

FREE! Harlequin Romance Catalogue

Here is a wonderful opportunity to read many of the Harlequin Romances you may have missed.

The HARLEQUIN ROMANCE CATALOGUE lists hundreds of titles which possibly are no longer available at your local bookseller. To receive your copy, just fill out the coupon below, mail it to us, and we'll rush your catalogue to you!

Following this page you'll find a sampling of a few of the Harlequin Romances listed in the catalogue. Should you wish to order any of these immediately, kindly check the titles desired and mail with coupon.

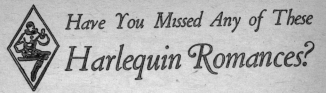

Have You Missed Any of These
Harlequin Romances?

- [ ] 1100 THE BROKEN WING
  Mary Burchell
- [ ] 1103 HEART OF GOLD
  Marjorie Moore
- [ ] 1031 FLOWERING DESERT
  Elizabeth Hoy
- [ ] 1138 LOVING IS GIVING
  Mary Burchell
- [ ] 1146 THE IMPERFECT SECRETARY
  Marjorie Lewty
- [ ] 1149 A NIGHTINGALE IN THE
  SYCAMORE   J. Beaufort
- [ ] 1164 MEADOWSWEET
  Margaret Malcolm
- [ ] 1165 WARD OF LUCIFER
  Mary Burchell
- [ ] 1167 DEAR BARBARIAN
  Janice Gray
- [ ] 1168 ROSE IN THE BUD
  Susan Barrie
- [ ] 1171 THE WINGS OF MEMORY
  Eleanor Farnes
- [ ] 1173 RED AS A ROSE
  Hilary Wilde
- [ ] 1181 DANGEROUS LOVE
  Jane Beaufort
- [ ] 1182 GOLDEN APPLE ISLAND
  Jane Arbor
- [ ] 1184 THE HOUSE OF OLIVER
  Jean S. Macleod
- [ ] 1213 THE MOONFLOWER
  Jean S. Macleod
- [ ] 1242 NEW DOCTOR AT NORTHMOOR
  Anne Durham
- [ ] 1307 A CHANCE TO WIN
  Margaret Rome
- [ ] 1308 A MIST IN GLEN TORRAN
  Amanda Doyle
- [ ] 1310 TAWNY ARE THE LEAVES
  Wynne May
- [ ] 1311 THE MARRIAGE WHEEL
  Susan Barrie
- [ ] 1312 PEPPERCORN HARVEST
  Ivy Ferrari
- [ ] 1314 SUMMER ISLAND
  Jean S. Macleod
- [ ] 1315 WHERE THE KOWHAI BLOOMS
  Mary Moore
- [ ] 1316 CAN THIS BE LOVE ?
  Margaret Malcolm

- [ ] 1317 BELOVED SPARROW
  Henrietta Reid
- [ ] 1318 PALACE OF THE PEACOCKS
  Violet Winspear
- [ ] 1319 BRITTLE BONDAGE
  Rosalind Brett
- [ ] 1320 SPANISH LACE
  Joyce Dingwell
- [ ] 1322 WIND THROUGH THE
  VINEYARDS   J. Armstrong
- [ ] 1324 QUEEN OF HEARTS
  Sara Seale
- [ ] 1325 NO SOONER LOVED
  Pauline Garner
- [ ] 1326 MEET ON MY GROUND
  Essie Summers
- [ ] 1327 MORE THAN GOLD
  Hilda Pressley
- [ ] 1328 A WIND SIGHING
  Catherine Airlie
- [ ] 1330 A HOME FOR JOY
  Mary Burchell
- [ ] 1331 HOTEL BELVEDERE
  Iris Danbury
- [ ] 1332 DON'T WALK ALONE
  Jane Donelly
- [ ] 1333 KEEPER OF THE HEART
  Gwen Westwood
- [ ] 1334 THE DAMASK ROSE
  Isobel Chace
- [ ] 1335 THE RED CLIFFS
  Eleanor Farnes
- [ ] 1336 THE CYPRESS GARDEN
  Jane Arbor
- [ ] 1338 SEA OF ZANJ   Roumella Lane
- [ ] 1339 SLAVE OF THE WIND
  Jean S. Macleod
- [ ] 1341 FIRE IS FOR SHARING
  Doris E. Smith
- [ ] 1342 THE FEEL OF SILK
  Joyce Dingwell
- [ ] 1344 THE DANGEROUS DELIGHT
  Violet Winspear
- [ ] 1352 THE MOUNTAIN OF STARS
  Catherine Airlie
- [ ] 1357 RIPPLES IN THE LAKE
  Mary Coates
- [ ] 1393 HEALER OF HEARTS
  Katrina Britt

All books listed are 50c.   Please use the handy order coupon.

B

GOLDEN HARLEQUIN LIBRARY

Now 24 Volumes!

Harlequin readers will be delighted! We've collected seventy two of your all-time favourite Harlequin Romance novels to present to you in an attractive new way. It's the Golden Harlequin Library.

Each volume contains three complete, unabridged Harlequin Romance novels, most of which have not been available since the original printing. Each volume is exquisitely bound in a fine quality rich gold hardcover with royal blue imprint. And each volume is priced at an unbelievable $1.75. That's right! Handsome, hardcover library editions at the price of paperbacks!

This very special collection of 24 volumes (there'll be more!) of classic Harlequin Romances would be a distinctive addition to your library. And imagine what a delightful gift they'd make for any Harlequin reader!

Start your collection now. See reverse of this page for full details.

GOLDEN HARLEQUIN LIBRARY — $1.75 each volume

Special Introductory Offer
(First 6 volumes only $8.75)

☐ **VOLUME I**
692 THE ONLY CHARITY, Sara Seale
785 THE SURGEON'S MARRIAGE
    Kathryn Blair
806 THE GOLDEN PEAKS
    Eleanor Farnes

☐ **VOLUME II**
649 KATE OF OUTPATIENTS
    Elizabeth Gilzean
774 HEATHERLEIGH, Essie Summers
853 SUGAR ISLAND, Jean S. Macleod

☐ **VOLUME III**
506 QUEEN'S COUNSEL, Alex Stuart
760 FAIR HORIZON, Rosalind Brett
801 DESERT NURSE, Jane Arbor

☐ **VOLUME IV**
501 DO SOMETHING DANGEROUS
    Elizabeth Hoy
816 THE YOUNGEST BRIDESMAID
    Sara Seale
875 DOCTOR DAVID ADVISES
    Hilary Wilde

☐ **VOLUME V**
721 SHIP'S SURGEON, Celine Conway
862 MOON OVER THE ALPS
    Essie Summers
887 LAKE OF SHADOWS, Jane Arbor

☐ **VOLUME VI**
644 NEVER TO LOVE, Anne Weale
650 THE GOLDEN ROSE, Kathryn Blair
814 A LONG WAY FROM HOME
    Jane Fraser

Just Published
($1.75 per volume)

☐ **VOLUME XIX**
705 THE LAST OF THE LOGANS
    Alex Stuart
740 NURSE ON HOLIDAY
    Rosalind Brett
789 COUNTRY OF THE HEART
    Catherine Airlie

☐ **VOLUME XX**
594 DOCTOR SARA COMES HOME
    Elizabeth Houghton
603 ACROSS THE COUNTER
    Mary Burchell
736 THE TALL PINES, Celine Conway

☐ **VOLUME XXI**
716 THE DOCTOR'S DAUGHTERS
    Anne Weale
792 GATES OF DAWN, Susan Barrie
808 THE GIRL AT SNOWY RIVER
    Joyce Dingwell

☐ **VOLUME XXII**
524 QUEEN'S NURSE, Jane Arbor
725 THE SONG AND THE SEA
    Isobel Chace
791 CITY OF PALMS, Pamela Kent

☐ **VOLUME XXIII**
742 COME BLOSSOM-TIME, MY LOVE
    Essie Summers
778 A CASE IN THE ALPS
    Margaret Baumann
848 THE KEEPER'S HOUSE
    Jane Fraser

☐ **VOLUME XXIV**
560 WINTERSBRIDE, Sara Seale
592 MARRIAGE COMPROMISE
    Margaret Malcolm
700 TAMARISK BAY, Kathryn Blair

To: Harlequin Reader Service, Dept. G.
   M.P.O. Box 707, Niagara Falls, N.Y. 14302
   Canadian address: Stratford, Ont., Canada

☐ Please send me complete listing of the 24 Golden Harlequin
   Library Volumes.

☐ Please send me the Golden Harlequin Library editions I
   have indicated above.

I enclose $_____ (No C.O.D.'s) To help defray postage
and handling costs, please add 50c.

Name _____

Address _____

City/Town _____

State/Province _____ Zip_____

H   GHL 372